A Beth-Hill Novel:
The Shadows Trilogy, Book 1:
Prince of Shadows

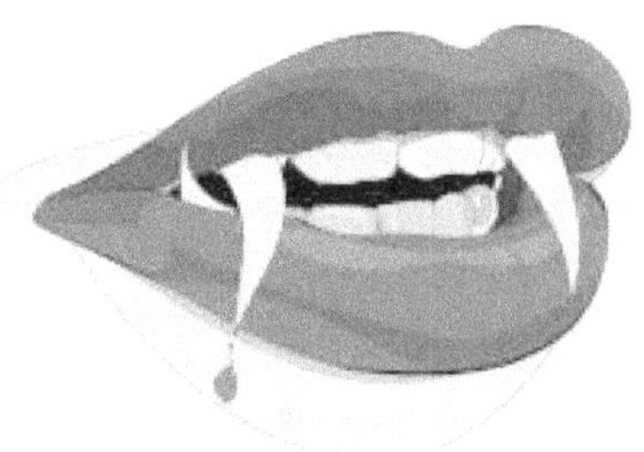

By Jennifer St. Clair

Writers Exchange E-Publishing
http://www.writers-exchange.com

A Beth-Hill Novel: The Shadows Trilogy, Book 1: Prince of Shadows

Copyright 2001, 2015, 2023 Jennifer St. Clair

Writers Exchange E-Publishing
PO Box 372
ATHERTON QLD 4883

Cover Art by: Jatin and Sandy Cummins

Published by Writers Exchange E-Publishing
http://www.writers-exchange.com

Dedication

To Chris, Mom, Dad, Emily, Bekah, and Jess
What more can I say?

Chapter 1

"Teluride, what have you done?"

The prince turned from his father's bloody form and stared at the spectre of his uncle in the doorway. Terrin's face was white--as white as the moon outside--and the faces of the castle staff crowding behind him showed no less horror.

"What have you *done*?" Terrin asked again, and, as if from some unseen prompt, the prince answered.

"My father..." His voice was rough and grating, his eyes unfocused. "My father..." He swayed, and nearly tripped over the bloody dagger at his feet.

One of the Council members pushed past Terrin and caught the Prince as he fell. Only the prince saw Terrin's face darken at this intrusion, and he was too dazed to make note of it.

"Help me with him!" The man lowered Teluride to the ground and turned to the onlookers. "Someone see to the King!"

Two more members of the King's Council pushed past, but it was evident to all that the King was already dead. No one could lose the amount of blood that soaked into the carpets and bed sheets, and survive. Not even their King.

"My father!" the Prince protested as the Council members held him down. "Help him..."

"I think he's beyond help," Terrin snapped, "and you've made sure of that, haven't you?"

One of the Council members gaped at Terrin. "Surely you don't think the prince..."

"He's been ill; we all know that," Terrin replied smoothly. "Illness can do strange things to a person's mind..." He left the actual accusation unsaid, but everyone present knew exactly what he meant.

"You're a wizard!" Another man pushed past the growing crowd and joined the others. "Can't you make him tell us?"

"*Force* him to talk, you mean?" Terrin asked, his voice still maddeningly calm. His eyes glittered at the thought. "I *could*, but it might damage his mind even more. If I forced a confession, whether guilty or not, he might not have a mind left when I'm finished." He paused. "I don't know if I want to do that to my nephew." His voice was perfectly modulated between sorrow for the King and worry for the prince.

On the floor, surrounded on all sides by the Council, the Prince moaned.

"Do it," one of the men snapped, his face pale as he faced the gory scene. "I want to know who did this to our King." The others, not as vocal now that the stink of blood and excrement was thick in their throats, nodded their assent. Terrin knelt beside Teluride, careful not to kneel in the blood, and the Council moved away.

"No! Don't hurt him!" Someone new pushed through the crowd in the doorway, and Terrin frowned when he saw who it was.

"Alban, step back," he snapped. "This is none of your affair."

"Teluride didn't kill his father," Alban retorted. "He couldn't have!"

"Perhaps the Prince's sickness has transferred to you?" Terrin asked, his voice still calm, but there was an undercurrent to it now, warning Alban from continuing in that vein. "You've been ill, too, Alban..."

"I'm not sick." Alban's face showed otherwise, for it was dreadfully pale, and his eyes burned with what looked like fever. Only Terrin knew it was not, but he wasn't intending to enlighten anyone. He *needed* his son; needed the power he carried. The fever in his eyes was a spell, nothing more, but no one else knew that.

"Alban, we found him here with the dagger in his hand," Terrin said gently, as if talking to a child. "I'm not one to accuse out of line, but the evidence damns him." His gaze promised punishment later if Alban kept interfering.

"My father..." the Prince whispered from the floor.

"Your father is dead, Teluride," Terrin purred, facing the Prince again. "Did you kill him?"

"Dead?" the Prince blinked dazed eyes, and tried to focus. "Dead?"

"Stabbed to death," Terrin said, almost conversationally. "Killed. By you?"

"No... I... heard..." Teluride struggled to sit up, but the Council held him down. "My father is dead?" He couldn't seem to grasp that little fact.

"He said no," one of the Council members said with a hint of relief. "He said no."

"Did you expect him to confess?" Terrin asked sharply, then immediately softened his tone. "Teluride, did you kill you father?"

"He's dead?" Teluride asked, nearly lucid now. "My father is dead?"

"Did you kill your father?" Terrin pressed, and backed his words with power this time. Teluride jerked on the floor, muscles spasming. He made a wordless sound of protest as Terrin focused more power into the question, but could not seem to speak. "Did you kill your father?" Terrin asked again.

Alban stepped into the crowd surrounding the prince. "You're killing him!" He tried to stop the tremors that ran through Teluride's body, but the spasms only grew in strength. Terrin's eyes gleamed.

"I warned you that asking him this might damage him in some way," he said. "I can't do a thing about the..."

Teluride's eyes widened, and he stiffened on the floor. His spine arced, bowing until it seemed his back would break, and the muscles along his arms and neck stood out in stark relief.

"You're killing him!" Alban said again, aghast. The Council members struggled to keep Teluride immobile, not wanting their prince to hurt himself any more than he already had.

"Go back to your rooms, Alban," Terrin growled, dropping all pretense of civility. "I'll deal with you later." Alban hesitated, obviously torn, but he could not disobey a direct order. He started to speak, wilted when Terrin glared, and staggered out of the room. The people clogging the doorway melted away as he passed by.

"Hold him still," Terrin ordered, and produced a small bottle from an inside pocket. "If I can get him to drink this, the convulsions should stop."

Teluride's eyes were still wide; his spine still bent at an unnatural angle. Terrin forced open his mouth, ignoring the damage he inflicted, and poured the milky liquid down the prince's throat. Predictably, he choked, but Terrin held his mouth closed until he swallowed the drug. Its effect was almost immediate. Teluride's whole body relaxed, and his eyes slipped shut.

"What should we do with him?" one of the Council members asked in the ensuing silence. Terrin pretended to think. Quite honestly, he wouldn't mind seeing Teluride hang for his father's murder, but hanging was a common man's death. Nobility would be sealed alive in a cell, or forgotten somewhere down in the dungeons. Or executed. He almost smiled at the prospect.

"Post a guard on him, but leave him in his rooms," he finally said. "We have to get a confession before anything can be done, and it's still possible he might be innocent."

"We saw the dagger in his hands," one of the Council members said darkly. "If he is innocent..."

Which he is, Terrin's mind supplied, but he didn't say a word. For his plan to bear fruit, Teluride had to be guilty. Teluride was the sacrifice for Terrin's quest for his brother's throne.

"Just make certain he doesn't start convulsing again," Terrin reminded them, and stood. "I'll prepare more medicine, just in case he does."

"Where will you be, Lord Terrin?" The Council stared up at him, already looking to him for answers. *This had been too easy by far.*

"I'll be in my chambers," he said. "Call my name, and I will come if you need me." He swept out, past the bloody form of his brother, past the gawking peasantry and Lords in the doorway, and past the deserted hall to go to his son's rooms.

Alban had nearly destroyed his plans by showing up when he did. If the Council found out that Terrin himself had killed the King, his plan would be ruined. If they found out Teluride's sickness was Terrin's doing, they would try their best to have him killed, but they would fail.

Terrin would make *sure* they would fail.

Alban staggered down the corridor leading to his rooms, unable to resist his father's order. He hated leaving Teluride alone with them; hated seeing his only friend helpless on the bloody carpet, but he couldn't fight the spell.

Now that he had his mind back, he knew it was a spell. He didn't remember much from the past month or two; his memories seemed to be shrouded in a darkness he couldn't pierce. He wasn't sure he wanted to pierce it.

He didn't notice the figure hiding in the shadows by his door until it spoke his name, but the spell still forced him forward, and he could do nothing but obey.

"Alban!" He recognized the figure now; recognized the cloaked form of his father's vampire, but couldn't reply until he'd stepped inside his room. He drew in a choked breath to cleanse the smell of blood from his throat, and sank to his knees as the compulsion deserted him.

"Alban?" A rustle behind him announced the presence of the vampire. "Where is Teluride? What is going on?"

"The King is dead," Alban whispered, winded without knowing why. He hadn't *run* all the way to his rooms, after all, but he felt strangely weak. Was the weakness part of the spell? Now that he had his mind back, would the spell still hold him?

"You're not free, are you?" the vampire asked, hovering in the doorway. "You're not free." Alban heard him turn to go, and turned himself, one hand out to prevent him from leaving.

"Don't go. Please." He felt like a fool for begging, but the vampire was the only one who could tell him what had happened. "I need to know..."

"You need to know nothing," Terrin growled from the doorway. He pushed past the vampire, and Alban tried to get out of his way. "How did you break free?"

"I'm not free," Alban snarled in helpless frustration. "I can do nothing like this. Let me go!"

"Nothing? You say nearly ruining my plans is *nothing*?" Terrin grinned at his son, showing even white teeth. "I will not let you go. *Ever.*"

Still kneeling on the floor, Alban stared up at his father in dismay. "Why?" He couldn't think of anything else to say.

Terrin smiled again, but his teeth remained hidden behind thin, pale lips. "You have power I need," he said simply. "And you are my son."

"And Teluride?" Alban asked, feeling despair well up in his chest. "What about Teluride?"

"He merely got in the way," Terrin replied. "Stay here. I don't want to see you set foot outside your rooms until I am crowned King. Do you understand?"

King? Alban tried to argue, but his mouth would only form two words. "I understand," he whispered, and bowed his head, defeated.

Terrin turned towards the vampire, and the cloaked form shrank back. "And I don't want to see *you* anywhere near the prince. Do you understand?"

"I understand," the vampire whispered. "You won't see me anywhere near the Prince." Terrin stopped in front of him, searching his shadows for any sign of deceit, but the vampire's head was bowed, his posture submissive. Terrin pushed him inside.

"Until I am King," he said. "Remember that." He wasn't looking at Alban, but Alban answered anyway.

"Until you are King."

The sound of the key in the lock echoed in Alban's head like a sentence of death. He collapsed, falling forward onto the dusty floor, and heard the vampire's soft voice break the silence.

"Do you truly wish to know what he made you do?" he asked, invisible in the darkness.

Alban raised his head. He had to work to find his voice, it seemed to have vanished along with his will to move.

"Yes," he finally whispered. "Please."

"You won't enjoy it," the vampire warned.

Alban waited a moment to see if he would elaborate, and then sighed. "I know."

Chapter 2

"My Queen? Have your heard the news?"

"Tell me how I could have heard the news, Mirror."

"You seem to know everything..."

"And don't try my patience. Not today."

"No, of course not, my Lady Skade. My Queen. I..."

"Your news, Mirror."

"The King of Leysan is dead."

"What?"

"The King of Leysan, King Valdis, is dead. His son has been accused of the murder."

"What did you say?"

"The King..."

"I heard you, Mirror, it was just a figure of speech. Valdis is dead?"

"Stabbed."

"And the Prince..."

"Accused of his murder."

"You're not a parrot; quit acting like one. And Terrin?"

"Terrin?"

"The King's brother, fool. Terrin. The wizard. The bane of my existence."

"He's...he's next in line for the throne, my Queen."

"Damn."

"I knew you wouldn't like the news."

"I never told you to only tell me good news, Mirror. What about Terrin's son? Alban? Isn't that his name?"

"Yes, My Queen."

"And stop this 'my Queen' crap. I'm not going to break you...not unless you really make me mad. What is my name, Mirror?"

"Skade, your Majesty."

"What did I... Oh, never mind. What about Alban?"

"Shouldn't you ask me 'what about the Prince?'"

"Shouldn't you have told me 'what about the prince?'"

"The rumor says he is dying. He's been ill, evidently, and he started to have convulsions..."

"Why is he being accused of his father's murder?"

"According to Terrin, he was found with the dagger in his hand."

"Of course."

"Of course?"

"I don't have to explain *everything* to you, do I?"

"No, My Lady."

"I like 'my lady' much better. Find me information about Terrin's son. And make sure the Prince isn't going to die."

"Yes, my Qu...my Lady."

"And hurry!"

"He put you under a spell," the vampire said, his voice echoing in the darkness. "A spell you couldn't break."

"I figured that much out," Alban admitted, and tried to rise. He made it to his feet, and stood there, swaying. "Is there a light in here?"

"You won't want a light," the vampire said. "Walk straight ahead. There's a chair beside your bed."

"Why won't I want a light?" Alban asked.

"You won't."

He heard the vampire move a chair and sit down with a sigh. Silence seeped into his ears and stopped up his throat until the only sound he could hear was the beating of his own heart. He closed his eyes in the darkness, stumbled forward, and almost fell across his bed.

"Sit down," the vampire ordered, and Alban sat. "You were under a spell." His voice sounded tired, as if speaking took strength he couldn't afford to give.

"I know," Alban whispered, "but what did he make me do?" He could almost see in the dark now; the light seeping under the door had enough strength for him to make out shadowy objects around his room. He saw the vampire, a darker shadow, in one corner, slumped in a wooden chair. He glanced behind him at the bed, and saw another shadow--a body-sized shadow--on the far end. His breath caught in his throat.

"Is this why I don't want a light on?" he croaked. He stood and started to back away from what looked like a body on his bed. But if this person was dead, where was the smell of decay?

"She's not dead, Alban," the vampire whispered. "Merely under a spell of your own making."

Alban stared back at him. "But I'm not a wizard!" he protested, trying to understand. "How can that be?"

The vampire sighed. "You have power," he said. "Power enough to make your father happy."

"I'm not a wizard," Alban said again, and turned away from the bed.

"You could be," the vampire insisted. "You could be more powerful than Terrin." Alban shook his head. "You could!"

"Who is she?" Alban asked, changing the subject. "And how do I break the spell?"

"Terrin gave her to you for sport," the vampire whispered. Alban winced. "He told you to do what you wished with her..."

"What did I do?" He couldn't even dredge up anger anymore; the only emotion lodged in his chest was a sick sense of dread.

"Break the spell and find out," the vampire suggested. Alban turned back to the bed.

He didn't have a chance to try to break the spell. The body on the bed rose, a dagger flashed, and he found it at his throat before he could react.

"Release me!" The dagger pricking his throat prevented his reply, so he took a step backwards, away from its sharp point. "Damn you!"

Alban cleared his throat. "How?" he asked, well away from the bed now. She stayed where she was, crouched low, waiting for him to return. Couldn't she escape from the bed? What kind of spell had he cast? *How* had he cast it?

She stared at him for a moment, confused by his question, then inexplicably began to laugh. Alban looked towards the vampire for help, but the shadow in the corner didn't even raise his head.

"You cannot free me?" she asked, still laughing. Her voice had an odd accent, one Alban hadn't heard before. "You cast a spell you do not know how to break?"

"I'm not a wizard," Alban said, for the third time. "I..." She laughed again.

"If you're not a wizard, then I'm not a woman," she snapped. "Free me, son of Terrin. Free me, and I swear I won't kill you."

"He doesn't know how," the vampire whispered, rousing from his stupor. "He isn't trained."

"For someone not trained, he cast a powerful spell," the girl said. "Light a lamp, spawn of Terrin. Use your magic. I've seen you do it before."

"I don't know how!" He shouted the vampire's words, and the girl's laughter died on her lips. In the silence, Alban bowed his head, staring at the floor again. "I am not a wizard."

"He isn't trained?" the girl's question was aimed at the vampire, but she regarded Alban like a species of new insect. Alban kept his head lowered, feeling both helpless and hopeless. He couldn't fight his father; he couldn't free the girl. And no matter what the vampire said, he *wasn't* a wizard.

"No." The vampire's voice cracked on that one word, and Alban slowly raised his head to stare at him.

"Are you..."

"Don't you dare ask him if he's okay," the girl snapped. "Don't you realize what you did to him?"

Alban's gaze swiveled back to her. "Did to him?" he asked, his throat almost too dry to force the words out. "What did I do to him?" She grew very still again, staring at him with that same peculiar expression.

"You don't remember." It wasn't a question, but Alban answered it anyway.

"No. All I remember..." He frowned and closed his eyes, *trying* to remember, but the darkness still shrouded the last two months. His last clear thought was being summoned to Terrin's rooms late one night. Everything else...everything else was covered with darkness.

"You..." the girl began, but this time, the vampire interrupted.

"Don't tell him!" the vampire nearly shouted, pushing his body out of the chair. "Don't tell him..."

"Tell me what?" Alban asked, feeling the cold lump of dread settle deep into his chest. "What did I do to you?"

The vampire sank back into his chair so quickly that Alban thought he'd fallen. He took a step forward, and one pale hand rose up out of the depths of darkness to stop him. "Stay back."

"What did I do?" Alban asked again, the anguish plain in his voice. The vampire did not reply, but the girl did.

"You hurt him very badly," she said, her voice soft. "Badly enough that I thought he might die..."

"I'm not going to die," the vampire whispered. "Not yet."

"And vampires are notoriously difficult to kill," the girl continued, as if he hadn't spoken.

Alban stared at her. "Who *are* you?" He finally asked. She laughed at him again, but her laugh didn't have the grating edge of before.

"You never bothered to ask me my name before," she said. "I'll tell you my name when you free me, son of Terrin."

"I can't," Alban's voice carried the depth of his defeat very clearly, and he turned away from her, towards the threshold he could not cross. She sighed.

"You *can*!" she insisted. "Look at me." He didn't turn. "Look at me!"

"I'm sorry," Alban whispered, still turned away. "I'm sorry I can't let you go."

"If I could escape from this damn spell of yours, I'd kill you myself!" the girl growled. "Come here. Now. Before I *really* get mad."

Alban turned and walked to his bed, his eyes still on the ground. He stopped within arm's reach of the girl, but she made no move to touch him.

"Free her," the vampire whispered from his chair. Alban turned on him, eyes flashing, his anger finally bubbling to the surface.

"I can't!" he shouted. "I'm not..." The girl grabbed his arm and pulled him towards the bed. Her dagger flashed again, and Alban found himself helpless with the dagger at his throat.

"Free me," she hissed in his ear.

He closed his eyes. "Kill me."

She released him in disgust and turned to the vampire. "What is wrong with him?" she asked, and aimed a kick in his direction. "He casts the spell, then says he isn't a wizard..." She spoke as if Alban wasn't there, and he almost preferred it that way. All he wanted to do was curl up in some dark corner and wait for his father to return. He slid down the side of the bed and sat there, head bowed, letting the conversation flow around him.

"He's *under* a spell," the vampire whispered, shifting in his chair. "And he hasn't been trained."

"Can *you* free me?" the girl asked.

The vampire sighed. "I could...once."

"But now?"

"Now I can do nothing," the vampire whispered. "Alban saw to that." He stared at Alban's hunched form for a moment. "*He* can free you. You only have to show him how."

The girl laughed. Alban felt her eyes on him, but he didn't look up. He wasn't sure if he could. "*I* am no wizard," she finally said, her voice soft. "How did he trap you, Alban?" This was the first time she had spoken his name, and he noticed enough to raise his head.

"I met my father for the first time two years ago," he whispered. "I thought...I thought he came back to be with me, to help King Valdis...I was a fool to trust him with anything."

"You didn't know," the vampire whispered.

"But you did!" Alban's eyes flashed. "Why didn't you tell me? I would have believed you."

"My counsel would have been suspect," the vampire whispered. "I am Terrin's, after all. I have no free will."

"What did I do to you?" Alban asked brokenly.

"What do vampires drink?" the girl asked softly, staring at the vampire, ignoring his whispered protest.

"Blood," Alban said.

"What *kind* of blood?" the girl asked.

The vampire rose unsteadily to his feet. "Don't tell him, damn you. Don't tell him!" The girl ignored him.

"Human?" Alban whispered, staring at the vampire.

"Vampires can only drink human blood," the girl said. "Everything else is poison to them. And you took his last resource away from him, and made that poison, too."

Alban stared at the vampire in horror. "I..." He tried to think of something; some platitude to say, but his mind was a yawning blank of blackness. "I..." He turned anguished eyes to the girl. "What did I do to you?"

She actually smiled at him. "You captured me after I had dismissed you as harmless. Other than that and this spell, you've done nothing." But Alban sensed something in her voice that told him she wasn't exactly telling the truth. He started to speak, but the vampire interrupted.

"It doesn't matter, Alban," he whispered. "What matters is that you learn enough to break your own spells. I can survive until then."

"And every time you drink, you die a little more," the girl snapped.

"Am I really a wizard?" Alban asked, looking up at him. "Could I break the spell I'm under? Could I help Teluride?"

"Teluride?" the girl asked. "What's wrong with Teluride?"

"King Valdis is dead," Alban whispered, still staring at the vampire. "Teluride stands accused of his murder."

"But..."

"He is innocent," the vampire whispered to Alban.

"Then who killed the King?" the girl asked.

Alban knew the answer, even though he didn't want to speak his suspicions aloud.

"Terrin," the vampire said, saving him. "And yes, Alban, you are a wizard, albeit untrained. You *could* break the spell you're under, and the one you placed on Kyne."

"And the one I placed on you?" Alban asked before realizing the vampire had spoken the girl's name. "Your name is Kyne?" She ignored him; her eyes were riveted on the vampire's dark form.

"You know my name." It wasn't a question, but the vampire answered it anyway.

"I do."

"And do you know why I am here?" she asked, her voice as cold as ice.

The vampire shrugged as best as he could. "I could guess," he whispered.

"And do you know *who* I am?" Kyne asked.

"Yes."

She seemed very dangerous suddenly, and Alban started to move away from the bed. Kyne noticed and grabbed his arm. She smiled down at him tightly, and he saw her clearly for the first time. Was there more light in the room? Had Terrin returned? He shot a panicky glance at the door, but it remained dark and silent. Only the space around Kyne and himself was lighter, but he couldn't tell where the light was coming from.

He stared up at her. Her black hair was cut short and spiky; her skin pale, but not sickly...not like his own. Her eyes were still dark, so he couldn't tell their exact color, but he thought they might be green. Her appearance was a marked difference to his own dirty brown hair and hazel eyes. Alban felt like a small, drab mouse beside her.

"Light?" she murmured, and looked down at him again. "Ah." She released him and settled back on her heels. "I rest my case."

"What?" Alban asked, then realized where the light came from. His hands were glowing--only enough to show him small details of his dusty room--but they were glowing. He moved them in front of his face, and green light swept through the air. "How is this happening?" he asked, glancing at the vampire for an answer.

He never heard the answer. The light winked out suddenly, and the darkness returned tenfold, pressing down on him from all sides. He felt his heart stutter, then stop. He tried to take a breath, tried to breathe, but his throat was locked and barred against oxygen. He tried to stand; to somehow move out of the darkness, but his legs would not obey him. He choked. He tried to scream.

And he felt as if someone sucked his very soul out of his body. He spiraled downward into darkness, with the sound of his own silent screams echoing in his ears.

Chapter 3

"Alban and Teluride. Kyne and the vampire. Terrin. Skade...and me." The voice was soft and dreamy, almost as if the speaker wasn't quite present.

"Who else?"

"I don't know."

"Dream the answer, then."

"I... I can't." Something shifted inside the wall--the Dreamer, perhaps--and the questioner glanced at his companion.

"Kyne isn't dead," she whispered.

"Kyne is alive, but trapped with Terrin's son and the vampire," the voice on the other side of the wall whispered, and the speaker saw impossibly *white* fingers poke out of the hole in the wall. "Did you bring food?" Only with this demand did the voice sound nearly aware.

"I did." The speaker slipped a bag through the hold, and the white fingers closed over it. "Is Terrin coming here?"

"He always does," the Dreamer replied, and the speaker heard it--Him? Her?--retreat.

"Wait!" The girl who looked so much like Kyne ran to the wall and crouched at the opening. "Wait..."

The speaker heard dragging footsteps return to the wall, and a small, white hand briefly touched his lady's gloved one.

"Kyne will not die," the Dreamer whispered.

"I'm not worried about Kyne. What about you?"

"Eadda..." the speaker warned. The Lady glanced back at him, her red lips pursed into a frown.

"You may go now, Doane," she said. "Wait for me by the horses."

The speaker, named Doane only by his Lady, started to protest, but a glare silenced what he wanted to say. They had ridden all day to get to this forsaken place at dusk, and he didn't want anyone to see them before they could return to Severin. He envisioned his home, pictured his warm bed in the castle, and realized they'd be spending the night under the stars. Eadda wouldn't want anyone to see them return. He gave her one last disapproving look, and went to wait out by the horses, trying not to let the Dreamer and what he represented dismay him too much.

"What about you?" Eadda asked again. "Will Terrin harm you?"

"Your sister awaits your reply," the Dreamer said, after a short silence. Its voice sounded different somehow, but Eadda couldn't pinpoint the change. Her sister was Queen of Severin, Cynara, and Eadda was the only one she trusted enough to slip into Glinyeu and consult Terrin's Dreamer. The news of King Valdis's death had stunned them all.

"My sister will wait," Eadda replied. "Answer my question, Dreamer."

"My name..." the voice hesitated, and Eadda saw a flash of murky movement from the other side of the wall. She leaned closer, trying to make out details, but she could only see a small shadowy figure, no details at all.

"You have a name?" she asked, surprised that she was shocked by that. Why wouldn't a Dreamer have a name? "What is your name?"

The Dreamer sighed, and the white hands appeared again, only briefly before they vanished back into the gloom. Eadda waited and heard a horse nicker softly outside the door.

"You have to leave," the Dreamer whispered, and she heard something rustle behind the wall. Paper? She leaned even closer, breathing in the scent of a closed off room. Around her, the ruined castle took on an air of menace. Eadda shivered. "You *must* leave."

"Is Terrin coming?" They were exposed on this hillside, and the castle only had so many hiding places, none of which would fit two humans and the horses. If Terrin came now... Eadda supposed they could beg for shelter at the new castle and try to get King Eabon to see straight for a change, but Cynara had been adamant about not being seen. If she'd messed everything up...

"No." The Dreamer's voice drooped with weariness. She saw the dark shape in front of the hole again, and this time, *she* reached through to it.

"Please tell me your name," she whispered, "and if I can help you."

The Dreamer sighed and touched her hand. "My name is Zaira. It used to be Zaira. Now go."

"Can I help you?" Eadda asked.

"Not now," the Dreamer replied, and she sensed a sort of fatalistic weariness in its tone. "If you don't leave now, you will not return."

"Will Terrin harm you?" The name 'Zaira' sounded vaguely familiar somehow, but Eadda couldn't remember where she'd heard it before. She would ask Cynara when she and Doane returned to Severin. Cynara would know, or would know whom to ask.

Just outside, nearly deafening, she heard a long, drawn out howl.

"You must go!" The Dreamer pushed her hand away, and Eadda stood. A thought struck her as she turned to go, and another howl split the darkness.

"We're not going to make it back, are we?" she asked, and heard Doane step up behind her as the second howl echoed through the ruins.

"Eadda..."

"Dreamer!" More howls answered the second one, and she heard the horses whinny nervously outside. "Will we make it back?"

One word. One soft, little word that turned Eadda's world upside down.

"No," the Dreamer said, and Terrin's Hounds attacked.

"Alban? Alban, can you hear me?" It was Kyne's voice, but with an unfamiliar edge of panic. "What's wrong with him?"

The vampire replied, his voice marked with pain now, as if holding the hurt inside no longer worked. "The spell. Terrin uses the spell to draw out Alban's power."

"Can he stop it?" Alban felt Kyne's hand brush his face, but he couldn't muster enough strength to tell her he was awake. "Can he really break the spell?"

"He could," was the reply.

"But he isn't trained." Kyne finished the sentence wearily. "I know. You've told me that before."

"It's true." The vampire didn't seem to want to argue.

"I'm not a wizard," Kyne said for the second time, mirroring Alban in her denial. "My arts are specialized and nothing that he needs. I can't train him."

"If you want to be free to return to your Queen..." the vampire's voice trailed off at the end, and Alban heard a sliding sound, then a soft thump as he hit the floor. Kyne swore under her breath.

Alban raised his head cautiously, expecting either pain or disorientation, but the room stayed where it was supposed to, and he felt no pain. He felt weak, dangerously weak, but he knew he had to see to the vampire, to see if he was alive.

"Alban?" Kyne's voice held just a hint of relief. "Can you stand?"

"I can crawl," Alban whispered stubbornly, and rolled over on the floor. He tried to get his legs to hold his weight, but they were too weak. His hands did not want to close over the edge of the bedframe, so he pushed himself on hands and knees to where the vampire lay.

In the corner of the room, a shadow that was not quite a shadow watched. Kyne was the first to notice it, and her hiss of alarm brought Alban up just short of the vampire's crumpled form.

"Who are you?" Alban rasped, struggling to his knees. The figure wasn't Terrin, Terrin wouldn't stand quietly and watch anything. It didn't move or answer his query, so he ignored it and concentrated on the vampire. The folds of black cloak were almost slick to the touch as he tried to find the body beneath it.

"See if you can wake him up," Kyne suggested. Her eyes never left the dark figure in the shadows. "Who are you?" she asked again.

Just as Alban touched the vampire's ice-cold hand, the figure spoke.

"You're not supposed to be able to see me," it whispered in a ghost of a voice. Kyne laughed.

"You appear in the room of Terrin's son, and think he won't see you?" she asked. "You appear to me, and think I would not sense you? Who sent you here?"

"How do you know I didn't come by myself?" the figure asked, a question for a question.

"I don't, but it's a good guess," Kyne said. "Who sent you here?"

"My mistress has an interest in Terrin's business," the figure replied haughtily. "She sent me here to find out about Terrin's son."

Alban raised his head, the vampire forgotten. "What about me?" he asked.

"See to your loyal friend," Kyne ordered, ignoring his question. "If I could do it, I would. Is he alive?"

The vampire's cold hand closed over Alban's arm, and he jumped.

"Alive," he rasped. "I'm fine...leave me be..." But his head dropped back into the pools of cloak again, and Alban found his fingers hovering over the vampire's protective cloak. He had yet to see the vampire's face. What horrors had his spell inflicted upon him? Or had he done worse, and marked him with the spell as well?

"Leave him be," Kyne whispered, her voice soft. "If he doesn't want you to see what he has become, then don't push him. Do you remember what he looked like before?"

Alban's eyes filled with tears he couldn't bear to shed. "I've only seen him without his cloak once," he whispered, and remembered the vampire's oddly naked face, staring at him in mute appeal as Terrin prepared to inflict a painful torture--sunlight--onto him for a transgression Alban no longer remembered. He should have realized then that his father would treat *anyone*, including his own son, like a slave. He held no bigger spot in his father's heart than did the packs of dogs he kept as Hounds. The thought was both sobering and sad, for he saw no way out of his predicament now.

"I'm sorry," he whispered, and felt the tears fall. He made no move to wipe them away.

The vampire's hand closed over his own in a brief, cold touch, then he was back in the chair again, moving too quickly for Alban to follow. That movement cost him dearly, and the knuckles of one white hand nearly cracked the arm of the chair to prevent another fall.

"He won't die yet," the figure by the door offered, "but he does need to drink..."

"I know what I need," the vampire snapped. "I have no need for you to tell me." He tried to straighten in the chair, started sliding again, and ended up on the floor beside Alban, knees drawn up to his chest, head bent down to his knees, white hands clasping his body so tightly that Alban feared his bones might break.

"Who is your Mistress?" Kyne asked, drawing the conversation back to the original thread.

"The Queen of Iomar, Skade," the figure replied, evidently expecting them to be impressed. Alban tried to remember where he had heard that name before, and Kyne laughed.

"Somehow, that thought does not comfort me," she said. "Why would Skade be interested in Terrin's business? And what would make her interested in Alban?"

"Please, Alban," the vampire whispered. "Leave me be. Go over to Kyne. I am not safe to be around right now. Please go." Alban hesitated, torn between tending the vampire and listening to the figure beside the door. In the end, listening won. He retreated, and left the vampire alone in the shadows.

"Who is Skade?" he asked, still confused. He knew he should know, but that memory seemed to be stuck in with the missing ones, and he was too tired to try to dig past the tons of darkness that seemed as solid as stone.

"Skade is the Queen of the island kingdom of Iomar," the figure replied. "She's been watching Terrin."

"Doesn't she have anything better to do?" Kyne asked, still scornful. Alban tried to stand again, and sank back down, defeated. He leaned back against the bed, near enough that Kyne could use the dagger if she chose, and far enough away from the vampire that the hunched figure in the shadows lost some of its intensity, some of its tension.

"Who are you?" he asked, feeling weariness settle into his bones. He could hardly hold his head up to look at the figure; he didn't truly care anymore what he had done or who the figure was. He only wanted to sleep.

The figure hesitated. When it spoke, the stiffness was gone, now it spoke the truth without varnish. "I have no name," it whispered. "I am Skade's Mirror."

"You mean you are *in* Skade's mirror?" Kyne asked.

The figure shrugged. "Either way. You're not supposed to be able to see me."

"And I'll say it again," Kyne muttered. "Terrin's son..."

The vampire could not hold back a moan as he unlocked his hands, lowered his knees and raised his head. Alban could see his eyes glinting feebly inside his hood, but he could not rouse enough to go to him.

The figure drifted across the room, and Alban saw that he really *was* a ghost--his feet didn't touch the floor, and he could see the faint image of the vampire's chair through the figure as he bent over the vampire. The ghost, Alban couldn't think to call him anything else, bent low over the vampire and murmured something. Surprised, the vampire whispered something back. Feeling like an intruder, Alban cleared his throat and desperately tried to focus.

"Why are you here?" he asked. "To free us?" He said this last question without much hope, for he couldn't muster enough strength to believe he would ever be freed.

The Ghost laughed softly and shook his head. "I would if I could," he whispered, "but I am powerless here. I will tell my Lady, though..." He flickered, then reappeared, fainter than before. "My Queen calls..."

"Will you be back?" Alban asked. The Ghost stared at him for a moment, then shook his head. Alban tried not to let his disappointment show.

"Kyne." The Ghost spoke to her directly for the first time. "Teach him how to free you before Terrin returns."

"Where did Terrin go?" the vampire asked, his voice harsh in the puddle of darkness.

"To Glinyeu," the Ghost replied, flickering again. "To visit his prophet." He vanished. Alban's shoulders slumped. After a moment, Kyne carefully put her hand on his shoulder.

"You can free yourself," she reminded him, but Alban barely heard her. "You can free yourself, and me, and the vampire..."

"Remember the glow before Terrin's spell sucked you away?" the vampire asked, his voice fading just like the Ghost's. "Remember, Alban?"

"Yes...but..." Alban whispered, doubt evident in his voice.

"You are a wizard," the vampire whispered. He coughed, and Alban stiffened. "No matter what your father made you do... Remember that. You *can* free yourself."

"I'll try," Alban said, still not really believing, even after seeing the glow coming from his own hands.

Kyne's hand squeezed his shoulder. "Turn to face me, then, Alban," she instructed, then lower, almost a mutter under her breath, "I hope you're right about this, vampire..."

For some reason, Alban felt better just knowing she didn't really believe she could teach him. He turned, faced her, and the lesson began.

The vampire watched, as always, hidden in the shadows.

Chapter 4

"My Queen?"

"Yes, Mirror? What took you so long?"

"They saw me, Skade. I didn't mean for it to be that way, but they saw me..."

"*Who* saw you?"

"Terrin's son. The Lady Assassin. The Vampire."

"*Names*, Mirror."

"Alban, Kyne..." a pause, "I don't know the vampire's name."

"Neither do I. But Kyne sounds familiar..."

"She's one of Cynara's Assassins."

"Ah. The Queen of Severin." A smile. "I remember now. She told me she was sending someone to keep an eye on things, but she didn't say she would send her own sister... Kyne didn't do her job very well, did she?"

"Alban is a wizard, my Lady."

"I know. His father is a wizard, so it only makes sense that he would be one, too."

"He doesn't believe he can free himself. I told Kyne to try to teach him, but..."

"Was he not trained?"

"Not at all, my Lady. Terrin placed him under a spell--it sucks his power from him to Terrin--and leaves him drained."

"How old is he, Mirror?"

"Sixteen? Fifteen? The prince is...will be, fifteen if he lives."

"Hmmm. And how fares the Prince?"

A wince. "I couldn't get through Terrin's spell to see him, my Lady, not even after he left. I tried..."

"Left? Where did he go?"

A hesitation. "To consult his prophet in Glinyeu, my Lady."

"His prophet? Is this the being Cynara told me about?"

"I believe so, my Queen."

"Hmmm! This is getting complicated. You'll have to try to see the Prince again, of course. I might pay a visit to a certain prophet..."

"Yes, of course, my Queen. I'll go right..."

"Mirror."

"Yes, my Queen?"

A sigh. "What is my name?"

"Skade, my Lady."

"Use it."

"Yes, my...Skade. My Queen."

"Mirror?"

"Yes?"

"See if you can find the Prince."

"Yes...Skade."

"But don't get caught by Terrin's spells."

"Can he do that?"

"If he can drain his own son, he can catch you."

"Oh."

"Be careful. And don't be gone too long this time."

"Yes, My Lady."

"What is this?"

Zaira opened her eyes at Terrin's voice, and knew he had discovered the bloated body of Doane and the remains of their horses. The wolves had killed everything but the Lady, and she had stopped moving around the night before. Zaira supposed she was dead, but she hadn't dared look out her little hole to see, and she had yet to dream about her survival. She didn't really want to see. The Lady had been so beautiful, so full of life, and the wolves had shown no mercy. She'd rather keep her last sight of her tucked up in the back of her mind where Terrin couldn't reach it, and call her image up when she wasn't seeing something else. She saw too much as it was, and the smell drove her back, deeper into the ruined part of what used to be a castle tower.

"What happened?" Terrin sounded both disgusted and angry. Zaira held her breath to keep from answering, but she was only prolonging what they both knew to be inevitable.

"They came," she whispered, her voice echoing in the dark room. "Came with...food and asked questions..."

"That you answered?" Terrin asked.

"You made it so," Zaira replied, the truth, as always. Terrin had made her a prophet. Terrin had placed the compulsion to answer questions, and Terrin had sealed her inside the windowless tower. Zaira hadn't seen the sun for nearly six years.

"And if I ordered you to speak only to me?" Terrin asked, without much hope.

"I have to answer," Zaira replied. It was an old argument. Zaira's presence wasn't widely known, but to those who looked in the right places, she was hard to miss. And a prophet who dreamed true... Prophets were rare things. Prophets who dreamed true and didn't surface with snatches of visions were even rarer.

"The Wolves aren't doing their job to keep idiots like these away," Terrin murmured, but since it wasn't a question, Zaira didn't answer. "Will I be King?"

Zaira hesitated. There were three possible answers to that question, and she disliked Terrin enough to give him the one that told him the least amount of information. But she also didn't want to be punished, and Terrin's punishments were always painful.

She settled for the second possible scenario. "You will be King, but..."

"But what?"

"You won't be able to kill Teluride."

"Why not?" Terrin kicked at something, and flies buzzed angrily outside the wall. The sour smell of death wafted through Zaira's only window to the outside world, driving her back into musty darkness.

Zaira hesitated again. If she gave out too much information, Terrin would demand even more. If she gave out too little, Terrin would more than likely punish her. "You'll want to pardon him for his crime. Say that he went crazy, and didn't know what he was doing." *But don't kill him before he can be rescued,* Zaira added in her mind. *Please.*

"But keep him under lock and key?"

You won't keep him long, Zaira thought, but didn't say that aloud. She'd realized a long time ago that she didn't have to tell Terrin *everything*. Pieces of everything; enough for Terrin to think he had the whole, but not everything. Especially with so much at stake. "Yes. Keep him locked up."

"What about my son?" Terrin asked.

"What about him?" Zaira replied, almost before she realized she had spoken. She held his breath. If Terrin got angry now...

"Will he escape from his room? From my spell?"

Zaira sagged in relief. "From his room...no." She could say that easily; Alban wouldn't exactly escape. He would...leave. "From your spell...yes. He will break your spell."

"Damn him," Terrin growled, then, "Is there anything else you want to add, Zaira? Is there anything you're leaving out?"

Zaira throttled the urge to tell Terrin everything. "No," she whispered, and hoped she sounded convincing enough. "Nothing else." Would it be now? Would Terrin open the secret door and take her now? She didn't dare to hope; didn't dare to let it show in her eyes.

"I can't quite leave you here..." Terrin muttered, and spoke the word that opened the door. Zaira scurried back as the door opened, driven back more by the smell than by fear. Terrin wouldn't kill her, not now, but she already knew when he would try.

Chapter 5

Alban was almost too tired to focus on Kyne's lesson, but he tried his best. He listened as she explained to him about magic and the supposed power he held inside a mind that felt like it had been stripped bare by his father's spell. He tried to concentrate when she showed him how to access his 'power', but he felt nothing stir in either mind or breast. His fingers remained stubbornly unlit, the spells unbroken.

"I can't do it," he finally whispered, bowing his head in what seemed to be a habitual position. "I can't even think straight, right now. I'm sorry."

Kyne growled under her breath, but she didn't take her frustration out on Alban. Instead, when she *did* speak, her voice was uncommonly gentle. "How long has it been since you've eaten, Alban? Do you know?"

He shook his head. "I'm not hungry."

"You're *beyond* hunger," the vampire whispered, from his place in front of the chair. "There's a difference. Believe me. I should know." His voice was ragged and thick, full of some unexpressed emotion Alban didn't want to think about.

"He'll use me again when he returns," Alban whispered, "and he might as well kill me this time. I have nothing left to give him." He closed his eyes and leaned his forehead against the side of his bed. "I'm sorry I couldn't free you."

Kyne wasn't listening. She rummaged around on the far side of the bed, and emerged with a skin half full of water. This she handed to Alban, who stared at it dully.

"Drink, Alban," Kyne ordered. Her voice had lost most of its bite. "It won't help you much, but it *will* help."

Alban's throat was almost too dry for him to swallow. He choked on the first mouthful of stale water, but what little trickled down to his stomach awoke a hunger so fierce that he almost couldn't straighten back up. He gasped and held onto his bed as a drowning man would latch onto a piece of driftwood.

"Hungry..."

"Once we get out of here, I'll fix you a feast," Kyne promised. "Unless you have a stash of food somewhere in this mess, water is all I have. I'm sorry I didn't realize how weak you were, Alban. I never should have tried..."

Alban focused his mind on the task at hand, and tried to ignore the pain in his stomach. At least it wasn't getting any worse. He felt something now, something that felt both familiar and strange settle over his body, almost like a favorite cloak once lost and now found. When he opened his eyes he could see a thin film of green light spreading across his bed, entwined with the very fibers of the sheets, trapping Kyne in one place for so long. It wasn't hard to break the spell once he knew what he was looking for, but it took the rest of his strength. He stretched out his hand and wiped away the sticky strands of green light, and heard Kyne gasp. A moment later, she was beside him, on the floor, gently lowering him to the ground. Alban dully watched the green light vanish into his skin.

"I'll get some food," she whispered, and was gone, out the door he could not open.

He lay for a moment or two, staring into the darkness that surrounded him, waiting for Terrin to return and see that the spell over Kyne was gone. Waiting for punishment, or death.

He drifted for a little while, lost in the darkness, until someone raised his head and put a rough wooden cup to his lips. And inside that cup...the most wonderful smell Alban had smelled in weeks.

He only drank half a cup of weak broth before true darkness bore him away to the shores of dreams, and he was powerless to stop it.

If anyone had noticed the travelers on the road, they would have thought it strange that a man such as Terrin would bring a child to the wilds of Glinyeu so late at night. The child was well-hidden in a bundled cloak too big for her slight frame. Neither the man nor the child spoke as Terrin's horse slowly made its way from the ruined and bloody castle to the newer one King Eabon had built six years ago, after the death of his only daughter. What houses there had been in between the new and old castles were gone now, a product of the war after the Princess' untimely death.

The Dreamer drank in the sight of the ruined huts and weedy road as if she hadn't seen civilization before. She had, but six years inside the tower had forced her to rely on memory instead of senses. She wanted to feel rain on her face, but the heavy storm clouds pressing down across Glinyeu did not grant her wish. Instead, they rode towards the new castle in a pall of darkness, Terrin grim and silent and the Dreamer riding behind him. Terrin didn't seem to be worried that the Dreamer would escape, and indeed, she did not even try. Her dreams had shown her what would happen, even as far as Teluride's eventual release, but she knew nothing would go as planned if she escaped from Terrin now. She had to stay Terrin's Dreamer a little while longer.

Her heart stuttered a little in her chest when the castle appeared on the horizon, and she tried not to think about the horrors that awaited her there. She huddled in Terrin's cloak, and brought up the image of the Lady Eadda.

Terrin hadn't mentioned seeing a Lady's body, and she thought that promising; perhaps she had gotten away somehow. Zaira knew she'd be rescued from Glinyeu sometime in the future, but she had yet to find out how, or who would do the deed. Waiting until she knew for sure would be hard, but she had spent the last six years waiting. She could wait for a little while longer.

When the stone walls of the castle closed the sight of the sky off, she felt tears gather in the corners of her eyes. She blinked them away.

There was death ahead; death and war and more of Terrin's plans.

The Dreamer, once named Zaira by her loving father, bowed her head at Terrin's muttered order, and tried not to think about what would happen next, but the dreams would not leave her in peace. They would never leave her alone. Terrin had seen to that nearly as well as he'd seen to his own brother's death.

Skade's appearance at the ruins of Glinyeu's ancestral castle would have given wind to many rumors if anyone had been out in the wet darkness to see her. Still, even though she took pains not to be seen, her bright red hair and vivid blue gown would have interested even the most sluggish of guards. But Terrin had posted no guards, and she saw no signs of his Hounds. She slipped inside the crumbled tower, saw the body of Eadda's Doane, and wrinkled her nose at the smell. And as soon as she saw the gaping hole in the Dreamer's prison, she knew she was too late.

"Damn." Skade stepped around the bloated bodies of Hounds and what looked like one human, and slipped inside the Dreamer's cage. The air inside the little room smelled of dust and mildew, and she stumbled over things more than once as she tried to feel her way to the back of the little room. As soon as she was certain no lights would be seen from the pitted road, she let one spring up from her fingertips.

There was a pile of rags in one corner...a bed, she surmised. A child's chair sat next to the pile of rags, and a small, dented kerosene lamp perched on the chair, empty of oil. A hole at the very back of the room, leading down into darkness too deep for her to pierce had been used, until just recently, as a latrine.

She uncovered a battered leather-bound book in her quest to learn more of Terrin's Dreamer, and found it was full of a child's crabbed writing, a diary of sorts that she tucked away to read later. She found the remains of a recent meal next to the chair, still wrapped in a silk kerchief that looked vaguely familiar. Skade frowned down at it. Where had she seen that cloth before? When nothing occurred to her, she folded the piece of cloth and tucked it away with the book.

Under the pitiful remains of the meal was a folded sheet of paper with her name on it, written in the same handwriting as the book. Skade frowned again, and picked up the piece of paper. It was from the book, torn inexpertly and ragged on two edges. The letter was stained with dust and grime, and looked to have been written years ago. It wasn't sealed so much as stuck together, and she tore the thick paper as she opened it.

Skade, she read. *I hesitate to address you so familiarly, since you are a Queen and all, but since you will tell me to call you Skade when we meet, I think you might not mind this once. I'm writing this letter in the hope that you will do as I ask. I cannot know that you will, for every vision of the future I've seen concerning you is blurry and not at all definite. Your work in this can be for both good and bad.*

I am Terrin's Dreamer. I saw you standing where you are standing five years ago, and knew Terrin would take me from this place soon after his bid for his brother's throne. I will not say I won't enjoy seeing new walls around me, but I do not look forward to what will happen to me in Glinyeu. I beg you to do as I ask.

You must send your mirror to Leysan, and make sure the Prince is still alive. If he is alive, take him from Leysan. If he survives, for even my Dreams are cloudy on this, he will need an army to take his kingdom back from Terrin. This is the only way he will regain his throne.

I have seen all of this, and told Terrin only what I am forced to tell him by his questions. Please, Skade, please help the Prince. I know he will die without your aid.

There was more, about Alban, the impending battle for Teluride's throne, and the mysterious vampire. Skade scanned the rest of the letter, realizing what she held in her hands. This could be the very proof she needed to destroy Terrin without having to resort to violence. If she showed this letter to the courts...Her eyes fastened on a small paragraph at the end of the letter.

Visions, although widely believed, are not admissible in a court of law. It is my belief that Terrin will not be stopped by any human law. I have not Dreamed the circumstances of his death yet, and unless he asks me directly, he will never hear the details from my lips. Please do not show this letter to anyone else, and speak of it only to your Mirror. If Terrin discovers what I have done, I will not survive to be rescued by you.

My name is Zaira. Do with that information what you will.

Skade stared down at the letter in her hand, then blankly around the room. Her mind saw the small pile of well-read books, the neatly folded clothing in a corner, the remnants of a life that was said to have ended six years before.

Anger momentarily turned her vision red, and she almost crumbled the letter in her hand.

"Zaira." She said this aloud, more out of fury than trying to remember where she had last heard that name. She already knew who Zaira was. "Damn him. *Zaira*." Something clattered in the passageway outside, and she slid the letter in with the book, instantly alert for danger. The only thing she was really worried about was Terrin's Hounds, and she'd heard no howls.

"Who's there?" She put every ounce of Queenly hauteur in that question, hoping to startle the presence into answering.

Rocks clattered down outside. After a moment, she heard a slow shuffling sound, then a voice, thick with tears and pain.

"My Lady, my name is Eadda. I was sent here to consult the Dreamer by my sister..."

"Cynara. Then these are your..."

"Doane was my man, yes. And the horses were mine, too." A bedraggled figure appeared in the Dreamer's doorway, her once beautiful face marked by pain and loss. Her clothes were tatters, mere shadows of the finery they once had been. "We tarried here too long, and the Hounds..." She sniffled. "I'm sorry, my Lady, I..."

Skade conjured a cloak and wrapped Eadda inside it. "Are you hurt?"

"Just my leg and my pride, my Lady," Eadda replied, and sagged gratefully in Skade's embrace. "I did not think Terrin would be such a diligent captor. I will not die from my wounds."

"I'll take you back with me to Iomar," Skade said. "You can contact your sister from there."

"I thank you, my Lady," Eadda murmured.

"You'll have to call me Skade if you're going to be my guest," Skade suggested. "Did you happen to see them leave?" She remembered the letter, and the name of the Dreamer, and new fury rose in her breast.

"Terrin and the Dreamer?" Eadda asked. "They left but two hours ago, heading towards King Eabon's castle."

"What did the Dreamer tell you?" Skade asked.

"Not much," Eadda admitted. "My sister sent me with a question, but she only said..." She paused, as if suddenly remembering something she had forgotten, and stared up at Skade, her face abruptly white. "Zaira! King Eabon's daughter..." She clutched at Skade, then released her and sank to the ground.

"Was named Zaira," Skade replied. "I know. She left me a...note. She knew I would be here, but she didn't know that you were alive, evidently."

"That poor child..."

"That poor child was said to be dead six years ago," Skade said tightly. "And Terrin fooled us all. You think they went to the castle?"

"Why? You don't intend to follow them there..."

"Not today," Skade replied, "but I'll be damned if I'm going to let Terrin have his way for another week." She remembered the words from the letter. "I have a feeling Zaira won't be in good shape when I get to her, and I don't want that to happen."

"What are you going to do?" Eadda stayed on the ground, adrenalin leaving in a rush now that she knew she was safe.

"For one, you will not tell your sister who Terrin's Dreamer is until I say it is okay," Skade replied. When Eadda made to protest, Skade shook her head. "This isn't my request. Terrin will kill Zaira if he finds out what she left behind. I don't want that to happen."

"What am I to tell my sister, then?" Eadda asked.

"The truth. Tell her you were set upon by Terrin's Hounds. Tell her you lost your man and your horses. Tell her I arrived after Terrin and the Dreamer left, but that I did not tell you why I came." Skade smiled. "She'll believe you. I'm not noted for my explanations."

Eadda managed a laugh. "That's true."

"Is that satisfactory?" Skade asked. "I understand you do not want to lie to your kin. I wouldn't either, but..."

"Yes," Eadda whispered. "If that will help Zaira, then I will not tell the whole truth."

"What was your question for the Dreamer?" Skade asked, realizing Eadda hadn't told her.

Eadda hesitated. "There are three sisters in the royal line of Severin," she finally said. "Cynara is eldest, the Queen. I am youngest. And our other sister..."

"Kyne," Skade said. "I've heard of her."

Eadda was visibly relieved by this. "Then you know what she does for my sister?" she asked. "She was sent to Leysan to...keep an eye on things there, and we haven't heard from her for over a month."

"And what did the Dreamer say?"

"That she is trapped, with Terrin's son Alban and a vampire, but unharmed." Eadda looked stubbornly up at Skade. "And that she will not die."

"She knew this, but she did not know if you would survive?" Skade asked. "I wonder how much Zaira actually knows. Is the future as set as one child's visions?"

"I would hope not, my Lady," Eadda whispered. She slowly stood, clearly exhausted from her ordeal. "Can we bury Doane? He served me well."

Skade regarded her for a moment, as if waiting to see if she would elaborate, then nodded. "I think so, but we'd best work quickly. I don't want Terrin to return while we are here."

Using a bit of power, she buried Eadda's Doane next to the crumbled tower. The horses she left where they lay. Terrin could take care of them, or send his Hounds to clean up the mess.

By the time they reached Iomar, dawn had broken over the Silver City, and Skade felt as if she'd traveled twice 'round the world instead of through two kingdoms. She sent Eadda to the healers, and locked herself in her rooms, intending to do some Mirror-research before getting some well-earned rest.

If Terrin really had outwitted everyone in the Seven Kingdoms, she wanted to know both how and why. She didn't remember much about Zaira-from-before, but she intended to find out everything she could before the presence in her Mirror returned and filed his report about Teluride, and before Eadda felt well enough to contact her sister.

She would not allow Terrin to outwit her again.

Chapter 6

"He will be returning soon. You should go."

It was the vampire's voice, but it was so faint Alban didn't recognize it at first. He lay still, not wanting to open his eyes or move limbs that felt as leaden as dead things.

"I knew the risks when I accepted this job, vampire," Kyne replied, her voice soft. "I can't leave now...things are just getting interesting."

"Then report to your Queen somehow, before all these interesting things die with you when he is under that spell again," the vampire snapped. Alban realized that this was the first time he remembered the vampire being angry.

"He isn't out from under the spell yet, am I right?" Kyne asked. "He freed me but not himself."

"He barely freed you," the vampire whispered, the anger gone. "I doubt he'll have enough strength to..."

Alban opened his eyes, and the vampire fell silent, the shadows around him growing thicker when he stopped moving. "I'll free you," Alban whispered. He tried to push himself up, but his arms would not support the weight. He closed his eyes again.

"I have more food," Kyne offered, "but I think you need rest more than food right now."

"I can't rest," Alban whispered. "I have to break the spell. If he comes back now, I might not survive."

"He's telling the truth," the vampire allowed. "Alban, can you see the spell?"

Alban lay there for a moment and cast his sight inward, trying to see what he had seen trapping Kyne on his bed. He saw only darkness, and slipped past murky memories of the past month; memories he didn't really want to set free.

"No." He saw no telltale signs of a spell. He could feel it...it ate at him like a cancer, spreading ice through his veins, and he suspected his father's spell was one of the main reasons he was so tired, but he could not see it. "I can feel it, but I can't see it."

"Then you will not be free." The vampire sounded almost resigned, as if he'd prepared himself for this possibility.

"I will be free!" Even Alban surprised himself with the ferocity of his own words. He managed to sit up and stared at the vampire. "I can't let him kill me. I don't want to kill you. And Teluride is my friend, unless I did something to hurt him, as well." That thought had not occurred to him until now, and he waited, holding his breath, for the vampire's reply.

"You did nothing to Teluride as far as I know," the vampire said mildly, but Alban sensed something in his tone that told him he wasn't exactly being forthcoming about 'nothing'. He decided to leave it lie for now. He had to concentrate on the spell, not on imagined crimes he might have committed.

"What do I need to do?" he asked. "Can I break the spell without seeing it?" His mind supplied, 'Can I break the spell at all?' but he tried not to think about failure. If he didn't break the spell, he was almost certain he would die. And although dying had looked good before, he no longer wanted to die.

Teluride needed his help. The vampire needed his help. And Kyne...well, Kyne didn't seem to need *anyone's* help.

"You should go," he said to Kyne. "I don't care if you leave or not, but you shouldn't be here when my father returns."

"He's right," the vampire whispered. "Contact your Queen, and tell her what happened. It may be the only way anyone knows what truly happened..." 'If Alban doesn't succeed' hung in the air as if he had spoken it aloud.

"I have to succeed," Alban whispered, but deep down in his heart, he feared he would not. He swung his legs over the side of the bed. "Kyne, please go. I don't want to be responsible for your death."

"As I do not wish to be responsible for yours," Kyne replied. "Why don't you both come with me to Severin? Cynara will welcome you."

"Your sister will not welcome courting Terrin's wrath," the vampire whispered.

"My sister can take care of both her borders and herself," Kyne replied. "I will leave immediately, but only if you're both with me."

Alban quelled the sudden surge of hope in his chest, and shook his head. "Take the vampire if you wish," he said bitterly, "but I can't leave. Terrin ordered me to stay."

"Then break the order," Kyne suggested.

Alban stared at her. "What did you say?"

"Break the order. That may be the key to breaking the spell." When he still stared, she shrugged. "You won't know until you try."

Alban turned to stare at the door as if he expected it to grow horns. "Disobey?" That mere word had enough power to make him shiver.

"I'll try to help you," Kyne offered. "I'll take your hand, and if we meet any resistance..."

"I don't know if that's a good idea," Alban whispered. His throat was so dry that it hurt to talk. "I don't think I can do it. I'm not sure I *want* to." Just the idea of disobeying an order from his father caused him to break out in a cold sweat. He slid backwards on the bed until his back was against the wall, and he could go no farther.

"I think the spell is making you act that way," Kyne observed. "You don't seem nearly as frightened of attempting to break the spell."

"I'm not..." Alban began, then realized he was clutching the bed sheets so hard that his hands hurt. He had to struggle to let them go. "If the spell is affecting me this way with only a suggestion to disobey, then what do you think it will do if I go through with it?"

"It won't kill you," the vampire said. "He doesn't want you dead."

Alban closed his eyes, and tried to quell the fear that wanted to race through his body and leave him a quivering wreck. He swallowed twice, hoping to wet his dry throat, but that only made it worse. Kyne took his hand and almost had to pull him up.

"If you're going to do this, you'd better do it soon," she suggested. "I'll walk with you. All you have to do is break through the spell."

Alban barely managed a smile. "I'll try my best," he whispered, and let her lead him towards the door.

"Why have you come here, Terrin?" King Eabon's voice was cracked and quivering, a remarked difference from when Zaira had last heard it. "I thought I told you to leave this land and never return."

They stood in the throneroom, alone with the King. No guards had met them at the door; no servants lit the lamps that hung along the walls. Zaira wasn't certain, but it seemed the King was alone in this great ark of a castle, alone and friendless. Remembering him how he had been before, Zaira almost felt sorry for the man who used to be her father.

"I brought you back your daughter, Eabon," Terrin replied calmly, his face impassive under his hood. Only his eyes belied how much he enjoyed baiting the King.

The man on the throne stared at Terrin, red-rimmed eyes narrowing, as if sensing a trick. "My daughter is dead." His tone of voice left no room for argument. "I don't know what kind of trick..."

Terrin shoved Zaira in front of him, and tore off the sheltering cloak. Even though there were no lamps lit in the room, the light hurt her eyes, and she fell on her knees in front of her father, nearly naked in her ragged clothes.

"That thing is no daughter of mine," Eabon hissed, and rose from his throne. "Get it out of my sight."

Zaira watched her father's approach through matted, moon-pale hair, trying not to shrink back on the cold floor. Even though she knew she would not die from this, it was hard not to beg for mercy, to throw herself at her father's feet, and prove to him that she *was* Zaira, no matter how strange she might look now. She wanted to feel his father's arms around her like they used to be. She wanted to feel safe and warm again, but she knew that would not happen here.

"Terrin! I demand that you remove this creature from my presence!" Eabon stopped at the edge of the dais and stared down at them, the very picture of a furious King, save for the matted food in his beard, the grease on his clothes and the madness in his eyes.

"My Dreamer needs a safe place to stay," Terrin said, his voice still soft. "You're nearly alone in this castle, Eabon. You can keep her safe for me."

"No." Eabon's voice almost sounded sane. "No. Never." He actually looked down at Zaira and shuddered. "I will not have your creatures here."

"But this is your child," Terrin replied, still implacable. Zaira flinched. "Will you not see her treated as a Princess should be treated?"

"My daughter is dead," Eabon replied. He sank down against his throne, all anger gone from his body, all strength leaving with the anger. "My daughter is dead. Take this *thing* away from my sight." He buried his head in his hands as if seeing Zaira hurt his eyes. "*Please*, Terrin. Take it away."

"Very well," Terrin replied, and his eyes seemed to glow in the dim light. Zaira felt him gather power, and tensed for a blow that she knew wouldn't come. "But she has to stay here, for now. You *will* feed her, and make sure she does not escape."

"I will." Eabon's voice was a thin shadow of its previous self. "Just go away, Terrin, and leave me in peace."

"Will he kill you?" Terrin asked, snapping the question at Zaira so quickly that she found herself answering before she could stop himself.

"No." She risked a glance at the man who used to be her father. "He won't kill me."

"But he'll hurt you?" Terrin asked. He sounded like he was smiling. Zaira didn't trust herself to look and see.

"Yes." Her throat was almost too dry to speak.

"You will not die?" Terrin asked.

"I won't die," Zaira whispered, truthfully, for she would be rescued before her father could kill her. But the pain up until then... She closed her eyes.

"Good." Terrin dismissed Zaira's fate with a wave of his hand. "I only need you alive. You'd be well to remember that. Get up." Zaira forced her legs to hold her, and staggered to her feet. Terrin held out the cloak, and she wrapped her body in it, effectively hiding her identity from any prying eyes. "Come with me."

Again, Terrin didn't seem to think Zaira would try to escape. She was almost tempted to try, just to see what the outcome in the future would be the next time she dreamed, but she lacked the courage to even attempt a change. She would have to hope that Skade would do as she asked, and that the one clear thread of the future she had seen variations, and shivered inside the heavy cloak. If it didn't, then beatings would not matter anymore. Hunger would not make a bit of difference, and she would finally be beyond the dreams.

Chapter 7

The Ghost from the mirror appeared in Leysan again, slipping through the shadows and Terrin's spell in search of the missing Prince. It wasn't difficult to find him this time--a mind in turmoil was as clear as the day to the mirror's sight--but the spells were difficult to breech. Not impossible to breech in any way, but difficult. When the Ghost finally won through the web of spells, he found the Prince lying unresponsive and alone in his own bed, eyes sunken and closed, the pillow under his head stained with vomit and what looked like blood. His skin was waxy and tinged with gray. His breath barely stirred the tattered quilt that lay across his body.

As far as the Ghost could tell, he had not been touched, or fed, since his father's murder. How long could he live this way? It had been too long since he was truly alive for him to remember hunger, and pain.

He wished he could bring the Prince food, but he was insubstantial in this form, unable to directly affect the physical world around him. He eyed the webs of Terrin's spells, especially the one that lay thick above the Prince, preventing him from rising even if he *did* awaken. Could he somehow remove the spell and take it with him? Free the Prince and please his mistress? He remembered her warning, and wondered if tampering with Terrin's spells was a good idea. What if he *did* get trapped? Could Terrin harm him in this form?

There was only one true way to find out. The Ghost of the mirror reached out one hand and began to brush away the strands of spell stuck to Teluride's face. At first, nothing happened. The sticky strands would not budge away from the Prince's face. The Ghost began to believe that perhaps his mistress had been wrong, that Terrin's spells *couldn't* affect him. He grew so absorbed in his task that he didn't notice when the strands began to weave around his own insubstantial legs, slowly drawing tighter and tighter until he had no choice but to notice he was trapped. He tried to struggle, but the glowing spell only tightened, drawing his shadowy form closer and closer to the mass of spells that covered the Prince's bed. He tried to vanish, to seek shelter back in his mirror, but he could not disappear.

His struggles grew more frantic when he noticed that the spell across Teluride had joined the weaving, forming a thick, multicolored braid that wove in the air in front of his eyes like a deadly snake. He fell back, away from the bed, as the spell around him seemed to grow teeth, sending jabs of pain into a body that had felt no physical sensation for many years. He tried to throw his hands up to protect his face as the spell-weaving inched upward, but the sticky strands caught his hands and held them bound.

He could not escape. Before the spell closed over his eyes, before blackness rose up to claim him, he sent a desperate cry for help to Skade, to his Queen. He felt something *shift* inside his mind, driving daggers of pain into his head. He heard something crack, and for a moment saw his mirror, neatly broken in two, with Skade's surprised face staring back at him through one half. The other half was blind and dark, as if he had lost the sight in one eye.

For one brief moment, he remembered everything--who he was, why he was Skade's prisoner--before ignorance blocked memories, and he was just a ghost again.

That scene wavered and became Teluride's lonely room, but this time, the ropes of spell lay twisting and dying on the floor, their color faded and their menace gone. For a moment he wavered between mirror and room, then he felt Skade's familiar magic take hold of him again. The Prince and his room faded. Familiarity returned, but it was tinged with redness, as if the very spell that held him to the mirror sensed his pain.

And for the first time since he awoke to find himself in the service of Skade as her mirror, the Ghost wept.

Alban's hand was on the door when something surged through the spell that held him, nearly driving him to his knees. He sagged against the door, saved by falling only by strength of will as he fought the spell that bound him, trying to wrest his freedom as the surge of power--he couldn't think to call it anything else--played havoc with his mind. For a brief second the darkness was gone from his mind, and he saw everything his father had ordered him to do, then it fell across the memories again and they were lost. He thought he lost consciousness for a moment, for when he opened his eyes he was on the floor, with Kyne's face staring down at him, and the vampire's voice whispering his name.

"What happened? Was it Terrin? Did he come back?"

Alban slowly got back to his feet. "I don't know what that was," he whispered, feeling strangely rejuvenated now that the surge of power was gone. "It wasn't my father." He gripped the door handle again, and took a deep breath, trying to clear the last of the cobwebs from his mind.

"One of your father's spells has failed," the vampire whispered, while Alban gathered the remnants of his courage. "When he feels that, he'll be back. You have to hurry."

Alban could feel time running out, almost as if he held an hourglass up against the power of the spell. He took one last look back at the vampire and Kyne, opened the door, stepped across the threshold, and fell to his knees as something--he supposed it was the spell--drove a dagger of pain deep inside his soul. His breath froze again in his lungs; his heartbeat stuttered. He felt the spell close down around his ears, pinning him to the ground, but this time, he found he had the strength to fight back.

He lacked knowledge, that much was true, but he did have power, he saw that now. He did have power. That meant Kyne had been right all along...he was a wizard. And he could fight back.

He felt his father become aware of his bid for freedom at the same time he saw the spell over the vampire--a twisted, hateful thing he broke without another thought. But battling a spell and battling his father were two very different things. He knew he had enough strength, albeit barely, to break the spell, but to fight Terrin himself... He would have to be gone before Terrin managed to return.

He pushed the spell away and felt Kyne behind him, reaching out to him as he lay across the threshold of the door, wanting to help but not quite knowing how. He heard the vampire's soundless scream as the spell around him shattered, and felt the spell around himself begin to crack.

He pushed until he thought he could push no more, and then he felt his father's spell begin to shrivel, lashing back at Terrin like a whip, driving his father to his knees in far away Glinyeu. He felt something split inside his mind, driving the pain so deep that he thought his brain would burst.

Thought and feeling returned slowly, seeping into his aching body like the survivors from a tornado venturing out in the light for the first time. He realized he still lay across the threshold first, but the door no longer held any power over him. As far as he could tell, the spell was gone.

"Alban?" Kyne's voice sent his head pounding, but he ignored the pain and raised his head. His eyes were tired and grainy, as if he'd been awake for days straight without any sleep. His entire body ached. He felt as if he'd been through a war. He licked his lips, but his mouth was so dry it didn't help.

"I..." He coughed. "I think the spell is broken." With Kyne's help, he was able to get to his feet, but his legs would not hold him. She lowered him down on his bed.

"You look terrible."

"I feel worse," Alban replied, and lowered his head in his hands. "How is the vampire?" He felt, rather than saw, Kyne glance over towards the vampire's corner, and her sharp intake of breath told him what he should have known before.

"He's gone. How did he..." Kyne rose from the bed and quickly scanned the room. "How did he get past you?"

"I broke the spell," Alban whispered, "He's probably starving. I don't think he's quite safe to be around right now." He remembered the hateful twist of the spell, and shivered. That he had been capable of that nearly made him want to kill himself so that Terrin could never control him again.

"Are you strong enough to walk?" Kyne asked. "We need to leave as soon as possible. Terrin could be back any minute now."

"The spell broke," Alban whispered. He only wanted to curl up and sleep for a week, but he knew he could not. There was still work to do, and he had to escape, preferably with Teluride. "He won't have enough power to return yet. And we have to find Teluride."

"Every second we stay here there's a chance of being caught," Kyne said. "I understand you want to save your friend, but..."

"I'm not leaving without him," Alban whispered. He managed to get to his feet and stood, swaying, barely able to stand. "I can't." He took a deep breath. "And I can't save him without your help, Kyne. Did you contact Cynara yet?"

Kyne's face darkened. "Yes. And I found out my younger sister Eadda is missing. She was sent to consult your father's Dreamer. Cynara fears the worst."

An image flashed through Alban's mind--an image of a ruined castle, and a small hole in a bricked-up wall. A small, pale, child's hand. And a voice... He shook his head, trying to focus on what they still had to do.

"We have to find Teluride," he whispered. "Do you know where he is?"

Kyne stood. "As far as I know, he's still in his rooms where Terrin locked him," she said. "But we have to hurry, Alban. If your father finds us here..."

"If my father finds us, kill me before he can trap me again," Alban whispered, and staggered out the door before Kyne could reply.

Chapter 8

"Mirror?"

Skade stood in front of what had been an ornate, full-length mirror, staring at the crack that had split it in half. In one half, the mirror showed her reflection, long red hair and comfortable dress, green eyes, pale skin. Some bards claimed her to be the most beautiful woman in the Seven Kingdoms, and Skade never said they were wrong.

"Mirror?"

The other half of the mirror was dark and tinged with red at the edges, and something that looked suspiciously like blood seeped from the crack in the middle. Skade touched the seepage and sniffed. It *was* blood.

"Mirror!" She poured power into the order, so much power, indeed, that the ends of her hair sparked with blue fire. The dark part of the mirror shifted, as if something--or someone's mind--sought to escape from her summons. And since she knew he could not disobey her, he had to be unable to obey. That did not bode well.

She had been in the doorway, talking to a serving girl, when the Mirror's scream ripped through the air, and the glass cracked in two. She'd been standing in front of the damage for an hour now, trying to get him to respond.

The mirror had just begun to bleed.

Skade closed her eyes and pressed one hand against the dark half of the mirror, delving into the prison she had created, searching for the mind within. She found only pain. That a spell of Terrin's would be able to attack a ghost was more troubling than she cared to think about. But she had warned him, and he had ignored her warning. She was half tempted to leave him there to die, but the mirror continued to bleed, and she really didn't want to have to clean blood off the carpets.

"Mirror, if you can answer, answer now," she said without much hope of a reply. When none came, she readied her spells, and spoke the word that would allow her inside the prison.

However much she would like to leave him to die, she had promised someone she would not. And Skade never forgot a promise.

The interior of the Mirror was dark and dank and smelled slightly of decay. Everything--walls, floor, and ceiling; indeed, the very air itself--was tinged with red, and there were spots of blood along the walls of the prison, testimony to Terrin's power. She hadn't even realized ghosts were capable of bleeding, much less pain. But where was he hiding? And, although it galled her to admit it, what would she do if he were dead? She'd grown rather used to having him.

"Mirror!" Her shout echoed off the walls, and the red tinge in the air grew a bit brighter. Did that mean he was close? "Mirror, if you can hear me, please answer." Silence. She gritted her teeth. "I only want to help you. I swear to you I won't hurt you."

A low moan, somewhere up ahead. Skade rounded a corner and saw him, curled up against the dead end of the corridor, so insubstantial that at first she wasn't certain the figure was the Ghost. As she drew closer, she saw more blood on the ground; great smears of red across the floor. His skin and hair, though normally gray, was covered, with seeping cuts and slashes. His eyes were closed.

Skade knelt on the floor beside him, ignoring the blood that stained her gown. Blood was much easier to get out of clothing than carpet.

"Mirror? Can you hear me?" One hand twitched at her voice, as if the spell she'd put on him wanted him to reply, but his eyes remained closed, and he didn't speak. She knew of one way to awaken him, but she wasn't about to speak his true name aloud. Even after all this time there were those in the Seven Kingdoms who would be very interested to know that their Prophet was a prisoner, and not dead as they believed. She could not risk it.

But she could do her best to make him comfortable, if he survived. Even though he was her prisoner, she would not leave him to suffer.

He moaned again. A frown briefly appeared on his scratched and bleeding face, and then vanished back into oblivion. Skade waited for a moment to see if he would wake up by himself, but he remained silent.

"Mirror, can you hear me?" Another frown. His eyes flickered behind the lids. "You need to wake up and tell me what happened so I can help you." She touched his cheek, marveling at the solidity of his skin. He was a Ghost. How could he have flesh here, in the prison? How could he have flesh at all?

As soon as she touched him, he awoke, his eyes snapping open, seeing something other than his Queen bending over him. He thrashed out and drew in breath to scream, but when he saw Skade's face, fell back against the wall. He did have substance here, she noted. Or was the substance all in his mind? The nature of the prison was such that her spell kept him hidden and trapped, but what if he'd unknowingly managed to find a way around her protections? What if he wasn't the model prisoner she thought he was?

"What happened?" Her tone was brisk, and she shoved all questions to the back of her mind. She knew her spells better than this, and she would have known if he had somehow managed to subvert them. He had been her prisoner for over a century. If she had her way, he would be her prisoner for a hundred more.

"I..." he coughed, and bright blood dotted gray lips, "I tried to help him..."

"Who? Teluride?"

The Ghost nodded convulsively. "There was a spell."

"I gathered that," Skade said. "And it caught you?" He nodded again, and let his eyes slip closed. "I warned you this might happen."

"He would have died," the Ghost whispered. "I had to help him."

"How do you know he would have died?"

"No one is feeding him, and the spells were so thick..." he coughed again. "I thought since I couldn't die..." This time, when he opened his eyes, she saw actual fear in them, not fear of her, which was usual, but fear of dying. And perhaps a touch of fear for Teluride?

"How do you know you cannot die?" Skade asked sharply, leaving her other questions for later.

He stared at her silently for a moment, and she decided she liked seeing him on the opposite side of the mirror more than face to face. Face to face, he reminded her of what he had done. At least in the Mirror he wasn't visible to her all the time. At least in the Mirror, she could forget about him for a little while.

"I didn't think you would allow me to die," he finally whispered. "Since I am your prisoner." As if she needed to be reminded about that.

"Even ghosts can die, too," Skade said. "He could have killed you just as easily as he could kill me." He stared at her, as if even imagining her dead were something utterly impossible. "He could have killed you. How did you escape?"

Confusion. "I thought you..." He stared up into her eyes, searching for something she knew was not there. "I thought you called me back."

This was new. She hadn't expected to hear that. She hadn't expected such loyalty, either, especially from a nameless ghost who was her prisoner, and would be her prisoner for the rest of his ghostly life. Was he that afraid of her?

"I didn't," she said, but he'd already guessed that. "I wasn't even in the room when the mirror broke."

"I saw your face..." He was still confused, but the pain had dulled any curiosity he might have had about how he had escaped. That was a shame, for Skade was still very curious.

"Mirror, I must ask you to tell me everything you saw and felt," she said gently. "I really need to know."

He tried to take a deep breath, but a cough cut off whatever he was about to say. "Why does it hurt so much?" He raised his bleeding hands. "Why is there so much blood?"

"I don't know the answers to your questions, yet," Skade said. "But I would like to help you, if you'll let me."

Now the familiar fear of her showed in his eyes, driving back the pain. It was more distrust than fear right now, but familiar nonetheless. "What are you going to do?"

"Well, you broke my mirror," Skade said. "You can't stay here, it isn't safe."

Awareness flickered momentarily in his cloudy eyes. "Safe for whom? You or me?"

Skade allowed herself a smile. "For both of us. A broken spell isn't something I want to leave lying around. And I'll need a new mirror."

"I'm sorry I broke your mirror, My Queen," the ghost whispered formally, and Skade thought she saw tears in his eyes.

"Mirrors can be replaced." Was she actually warming towards him? She found she felt sorry for him, and was mildly surprised. This was her prisoner, the most dangerous one she held captive. This was the traitor, the self-proclaimed prophet who had looked the other way as his followers were murdered. Why should she feel sorry for him *now*?

"I only wanted to help the Prince," he whispered, and let his head fall back against the wall. "I only wanted to help him." His eyes slowly closed.

And then she realized why. He'd never, *ever* tried to do something for someone else before. He had been in the mirror for over a century, and doing her bidding for nearly fifty years. *But he had not tried to help anyone before.* Was the prophet finally gaining a conscience? Would she eventually be able to free him? She doubted that, but perhaps that time would come.

"Will you let me help you?" Skade asked, her voice uncommonly soft. Perhaps he heard something in her voice; perhaps he no longer cared what she would do to him.

"Yes." He did not open his eyes. "I'm sorry."

"It is I who should be sorry," Skade whispered, although she didn't think he could hear her anymore. "I sent you there without any protections. It will not happen again."

She lifted his insubstantial form, cradling his head against one shoulder, and carried him out of the mirror and into her rooms.

"This will be your room."

Zaira peeked out from behind Terrin and saw luxury, compared to what she was used to. The room was tiny, almost a closet, but there was a real bed, and clean enough sheets. There was even a tiny window set high up in the wall.

"You won't be here for long," Terrin said. "I'll make a room for you in Leysan. That way, no one else can hear of your dreams."

Zaira hesitated in the doorway, remembering her dream, trying not to think of what would happen to her in this room.

Terrin pushed her inside. "I'll see to it that your father feeds you. And I'll be back in a few days to hear your dreams."

I might be dead in a few days, Zaira thought, but pushed the thoughts of death from her mind. If everything went well, she wouldn't die, and she would be rescued. *If* everything went well.

Terrin was halfway out the door when a surge of power swept through the room and slammed into his back. He staggered and almost fell, but caught himself against the door. Zaira stood and stared. She had never seen Terrin weak before. She had never seen Terrin stagger back from *anything*.

He stood for a moment, clinging to the door, breathing hard, his face nearly as pale as Zaira's, before his eyes opened and fixed on his unfortunate Dreamer. "*Did you know this would happen?*" he rasped, anger burning away the aftereffects of the broken spell.

Zaira stepped back, arms raised to shield her face from any blows. "I knew he would escape from the spell, I told you that..." When Terrin stepped away from the door to go after her, he almost fell. Zaira scuttled back anyway, not wanting to get hit.

"You didn't tell me it would affect me like *this!*" Two spots of color burned high in Terrin's cheeks, and his eyes glittered dangerously. Zaira didn't even try to look around for a way to escape. She already knew there was none.

"I told you everything I knew!" she whispered, still backing away. When she hit the bed, she stopped, staring at Terrin, waiting to die.

Terrin took one step inside the room, then turned on his heel and swept out, stumbling a little in his haste to leave. He turned at the door. "If I have to ride back to Leysan because I cannot use magic, I will be *very* angry with you, Zaira."

Zaira stood silent, rooted to the floor, her eyes wide. Only after Terrin had gone and locked the door behind him, did she allow himself to sink on the bed. She had *not* seen this. She had not seen Terrin nearly collapsing because of the spell.

What else hadn't she seen?

She scooted back against the wall and lay on the bed, keeping her eyes on the door. Even though Terrin had locked the door, she knew her father had keys to all the doors in the castle, and she wanted to be ready when Eabon came for her.

Time passed. She watched the sun rise as much as she could from the high window, and heard Terrin leave soon after, on a horse. The silence of the little room rocked her to sleep, and she fell away into darkness, too tired to wait for her father to arrive.

Too tired to worry about death.

When she awoke, with late afternoon sun shining high on the wall and the rest of the room cold and dark, Eabon stood in the doorway, red-rimmed eyes focused on the child that was once his daughter.

Zaira froze, eyes stinging from the unaccustomed light, even though Eabon probably needed a torch to see her clearly. Her father didn't move.

"Are you really my daughter?" he finally asked, his voice loud in the silence.

Zaira stared at him for a moment, trying to gauge what his reaction would be to the answer. She had no choice but to answer. Terrin had seen to that. She closed his eyes.

"Yes."

Silence came from the doorway for so long that Zaira thought her father had left her. But when she opened her eyes, Eabon still stood in the doorway, staring.

"And Terrin did this to you?"

"Yes."

Eabon turned away. Zaira could almost taste his disgust, and tried not to let it show. "And you Dream for him? *You* are the creature in the tower?"

"Yes." Zaira's voice was barely audible. She felt slightly sick, and wondered dully if she would feel like that until her father tried to murder her.

"And I am to feed you, knowing this?" He shook his head. "You'll get no food from me."

"I know."

Eabon turned and gave her a look that was almost sane. "And what else do you know?" he asked. "Do you truly tell the future, or is this just a sham?"

Again, a question she had to answer.

"I tell the truth," she whispered. "I tell what I see."

Eabon stared at him. "And what do you see when you look into my future?" he asked. His voice was flat, as if he didn't truly believe Zaira would answer.

Zaira closed her eyes. "Your death," she whispered.

There was a stunned sort of silence from across the room. "My *what?*" Eabon finally asked, as if he couldn't quite believe what Zaira had said.

"Your death."

Eabon moved quickly, despite his apparent lack of strength. He was across the room in a moment, lifting Zaira off the bed and slamming her against the wall. "My what?" Spittle sprayed in Zaira's face.

"I saw your death," Zaira whispered, not even trying to struggle. Eabon released her. She collapsed on the soft mattress and tried not to think about how it would soon be covered with blood. Her blood. She opened her eyes, and saw Eabon turn away. She almost relaxed, thinking that the pain would come later, but her father turned back to her and swept a dagger through the air right in front of her face. Zaira bit back a shriek.

"What kind of death did you see?" Eabon asked, his voice deadly soft. The glint of madness in his eyes was now full-blown, driving back any sense he might have had remaining. He pressed the dagger against Zaira's throat, nearly lying full-length on his daughter. Zaira stared into her father's eyes and saw her own death. She almost let it happen.

Almost.

She managed to push away from the dagger, nicking one hand in the process, but she hardly felt the pain. Eabon let her squirm away--now that he had seen Zaira clearly, he didn't want to be that close to the creature that once was his only child.

"What did you see?"

Zaira wanted to close her eyes. She wanted to curl up in the bed and forget everything she had seen, but she knew Eabon wouldn't let her. Se knew what would happen if she refused to answer.

"Terrin will kill you," Zaira whispered. "And you will be buried in a pauper's grave." The blow came too fast for her to dodge. The dagger's hilt and her father's fist slammed into the side of Zaira's head, sending her rocking back against the wall. Another blow followed the first, then another, then another. Zaira didn't have enough strength to try to defend herself. And after a little while, it seemed better to drift away from the pain; away from the dreams that ruled her life, and let her father have his way.

When Eabon staggered out of the room fifteen minutes later, the dagger lay on the floor, nearly lost under the bed, and Zaira lay on the bloodstained sheets, bruises already purpling her pale skin.

And for once, the Dreamer did not dream.

Chapter 9

When he awoke, he did not know who he was, or how he came to be in this dark, cold place. He could not remember his name or his crime--for he had to have committed a terrible crime to be locked down in this darkness. He tried to rise, but his body seemed to be locked in place, either by chains or by drugs. He couldn't feel anything but the cold that seemed to have settled into his bones.

Was he dead? Had some sickness killed him, leaving his spirit intact? Had he been buried and left to rot? Panic surged through his body, burning off most of the numbness. He felt coarse cloth under him and a stiff pillow under his head. He heard his breath loud in his ears, and finally, a heartbeat.

He wasn't dead. Relief washed over him in a flood, nearly sending him back down into the darkness again. If he wasn't dead, then why was he here? What was his name? His fingers twitched, sending pain streaking up his entire arm. The darkness slowly melted away, and he saw shadowy things around him, telling him that he was not in a dungeon cell as he had first thought, but that he was in someone's room. His own? The dim shapes he saw held no memories; no place in his heart. Even the bed he lay on was a mystery.

He tried to rise again, and felt blackness rise up to shroud him, beating consciousness back down as if it weighed nothing. He collapsed back onto the bed, panting, his breath loud in his ears. Perhaps he would lie still for a little while longer. Perhaps, then, his memories would return, and he would know why he hurt so, and why every muscle in his body felt as if it had been stretched too tightly, and all at once.

Ever-so-slowly, feeling returned to his body, inching up his legs, awakening pains he had no idea existed. He managed to rotate his head on the stiff pillow and look towards the door...it remained shut and silent, telling him nothing. He managed to raise one arm, biting back a whimper at the pain, and to touch his face, as if touch alone would tell him his identity. All he felt was clots of dried blood and hardened vomit. He brushed as much of it away as he could before his strength gave out on him.

His mouth ached when he managed to open it, and he felt scabs tear along the sides of his lips. He tried to wet his dry mouth, to somehow remember how to speak, but his tongue was as dry as a desert, and did nothing for his sudden thirst.

Thirst, and hunger. As soon as his body fully awoke, his stomach growled, causing him to wonder how long it had been since he had eaten. Had he been left to die here? He would never know if his memories did not return, and they showed no sign of coming back. His mind was still blank, as clear as a wiped clean slate. He felt the first bubbling of panic in his breast.

A new sound intruded, a real sound, not one of his own making. As he watched, held immobile by pain and terror, the door slowly swung open, and a figure slipped inside. It was a dark figure, hidden by a cloak, its hand on the door almost glowing in the darkness. It closed the door behind it, turned, and froze when it saw he was awake.

He tried to speak, but he could only manage a harsh croaking question of a sound. It wasn't even close to true speech, but the figure seemed to understand.

"I'm very glad you're awake," it whispered, and slowly made its way to his bed. "Do you remember what happened? Are you wounded?"

He tried again, struggling to force words past the blockage in his throat. This time, he couldn't even manage a sound.

The figure held up a waterskin. "I thought you might be thirsty," it whispered, and he sensed some sort of feeling in its voice, almost as if it had just survived a deadly sickness. Almost as if it, too, had faced death and survived.

The first mouthful of water nearly made him choke, but he forced it down and swallowed more. What didn't make it into his mouth slowly rinsed off his face, and when he finally stopped drinking, he felt more clearheaded than ever, except for the fact that his memories were still gone.

But would he be able to speak?

He opened his mouth. "Who...are you?"

The figure stepped back, and he had a feeling that it regarded him strangely; as if he had asked a question he should have known the answer to.

He tried again. "Who...am I?"

This time, he clearly heard the figure curse. It lay the waterskin down beside him on the bed and pulled up a small stool. Up close, the shadows around its face weren't as dark, but he still could not see it clearly.

"You don't know who I am?" it asked. Shaking his head seemed to be beyond him, so he wet his lips and managed a hoarse 'no'. "Or who you are?"

This time, he just stared. The figure sighed and lowered its head to its hands. When it lifted its head, it pulled off the hood, showing him lank black hair and pale, pale skin. That skin was drawn tightly over the figure's bones, making his face seem like a living skull. His eyes were blue and ringed with shadows. "You don't recognize me."

"No."

At least, with practice, his voice seemed to be getting stronger.

"Damn him!" The figure drew his hood back over his head, and sat in shadows again, staring at nothing.

"Damn who?"

"Your name is Teluride." That name meant nothing to him, but he clutched at it anyway, wanting some sort of substance in his head. "You're a prince. You're here..." He sighed. "Don't worry why you're here right now. I'll tell you about it after Alban gets here to rescue you."

"A-Alban?" That name seemed vaguely familiar, but he could place no more significance to it. "Who are you?"

"I..." for once, the figure seemed at a loss for words, "I have no name, Teluride. Your uncle--the one who holds you here--stole it from me a long time ago."

"Then what do I call you?" Teluride asked. He managed to raise one hand as the figure turned to glance at the door, and found the white skin nearly freezing to the touch. The figure snatched its hand away.

"I don't think you've ever called me anything," he whispered. "Lie still and rest. I'll be right back."

"No!" His voice was louder than he expected, and echoed through the room. Teluride tried to push his aching body up, and nearly barreled downward into darkness again. "Please don't leave me here..."

"I'm not leaving." The figure's voice was almost gentle. "Lie back, Teluride. I will not leave this room."

Teluride lay back and closed his eyes. "What shall I call you?" he finally asked, hoping the figure had kept his word and not left the room.

"Your uncle calls me 'vampire'," the vampire replied, his voice a mere ghost in the darkness. "That will do as well as any."

Teluride's eyes snapped open. Vague memories swirled through his head as he stared at the dark figure by the door; confusing and disjointed memories he couldn't keep straight. "*Vampire?*" he whispered, trying to remember why that one word sent shivers up his spine. There was a chuckle from the darkness.

"I'll let you sort it out yourself, when you regain your memories," the vampire whispered. "But be assured you have nothing to fear from me."

"What if my memories don't come back?" Teluride asked, voicing the question that would not leave his mind.

The vampire sighed. "They will. Even *Terrin* isn't that powerful."

Terrin had to be his uncle, then. Teluride lay back in his bed and probed the empty spaces in his mind, trying to force his memories to return.

He only got a headache for his trouble.

Terrin was still slightly weak from the spell's destruction, but he knew he had to reach Leysan before Alban escaped, and he was in no mood to wait for his strength to return to him. He did not want to leave Zaira alone in Eabon's castle, but he had no true choice. Bringing his Dreamer with him to Leysan would start rumors he didn't want to hear. Holding onto the throne would be difficult enough without Alban's power to aid him. Holding onto the throne would be near to impossible if Teluride were to escape.

He had no doubt that Alban would attempt to rescue Teluride, but he couldn't believe his son had managed to break all the spells he'd put over the Prince. He had felt a surge in those spells a little while ago, but that had been before Alban's bid for freedom; before the damned spell erupted in his face.

He began to regret even coming to Glinyeu. Zaira had not told him anything he didn't already know, and it seemed his plans were unraveling the longer he stayed away from his rightful throne. He gritted his teeth and rode on, nearly past the now-empty tower, and realized the bodies would have to be dealt with, or there would be rumors.

"Damn." He turned his horse to the tower and dismounted, hurrying through clouds of black flies, gathering what little magic remained to burn the bodies and Zaira's little room, so that no one could find any evidence of wrongdoing.

He stopped at the edge of the carnage, gaze riveted on the torn bodies...or, more specifically, the body that was no longer there.

He growled a spell under his breath, but could find no telltale sign of magic, no trace of anyone's presence but his own, Zaira's, the missing body, and one other person. A woman. Terrin growled under his breath. There were two horses, why hadn't he seen that before? The man had not been alone. Someone had seen him take Zaira to Glinyeu, and someone had evidently come back and either stolen or buried the body. And he had not thought to look for survivors.

What would that mean to his plans? Whoever the survivor was, she was probably long gone, and he had little hope of finding her identity from the trace that remained of her presence, especially since he did not have the full use of his powers. He growled again. Why hadn't he realized there had been two questioners before? Why hadn't Zaira told him? What else had Zaira lied about?

If he hadn't needed to get back to Leysan quickly and punish his son, he would have returned to Glinyeu to punish Zaira. He would have to deal with Zaira later. Alban's powers were much more important right now. He swung back up on his horse and spoke the spell to burn all traces of his Dreamer into dust. Flames licked around the tumbled stones as he rode away.

Chapter 10

The Ghost opened his eyes, and found he lay on Skade's bed, his gray skin contrasting sharply with her colorful quilts. The colorful quilts were now dotted with blood; blood that should not truly exist. How could he bleed if he were truly a ghost? How could he hurt so badly? He twisted his head towards where the mirror should have been, and found it strange to see it from the other side. It no longer hung on the wall but leaned against it, cracked and broken, the spell obviously gone. He felt nothing from it; no tugging, no sense that he belonged inside of it. He wondered how long that feeling would last. How long would she leave him free?

He knew he was not truly free, but being outside the cold world of the mirror felt like freedom to one who had been a prisoner for so long. He only wished he could feel the quilts under him. He was a little surprised that his body hadn't faded through the entire bed and deposited him on the floor, but he seemed to be fairly solid here, at least on her bed. He decided not to try to rise.

"Ah. You're awake." Her voice was perfect and lovely, stroking his skin like a lover's touch. Skade appeared beside the bed, her dress now spotless, and her hair shining and spotted with beads. "How do you feel?"

He considered her question very carefully. "Better." And the questions, so bright and burning in his mind, had to be voiced. "How can I be here if I am a ghost? How could I be hurt by Terrin's spells? *How can I bleed?*" He stopped as soon as he realized how he was speaking to his Queen; his jailer, and turned his head away from her. She owed him no answers. She had saved what life he had, but she owed him nothing. This time, his voice was quieter, more like the whisper of old. "Thank you for saving my life, My Lady."

Skade stared at him for a moment, as if she expected him to say more, but he kept his face averted, his gaze downcast.

"Wouldn't you like answers to your questions?" she asked.

He still wouldn't look at her. "I didn't think you would answer them," he admitted, his voice nearly inaudible.

She sat down beside him, her chin cupped in one hand. "I don't think I would have, if this had happened yesterday." Her voice was frank, and not at all like her usual tone. He forgot himself enough to glance up at her, and found himself helplessly trapped in her gaze. "But you did something for someone else, and that does at least warrant answers to your questions."

"But did I succeed?" He remembered seeing the spells around the Prince's body, and shuddered on her bed. "Did I remove the spells?"

"Even worse," Skade replied. "You brought them back here with you." She stood. "Your prison is whatever your mind wants to make of it, Mirror. If you expect me to lock you in a tiny cell, then it would be a tiny cell. If you expect riches, then that's what you would receive. If you expect to bleed after hurting so much, then you will bleed."

"And if I expect death?" The question appeared out of nowhere, startling him. He stared up at her, stricken.

She sighed. "I cannot alter what you will see. If you expect death, then you may die. There are no guarantees."

She'd never been so frank with him before, and he found his fear of her thawing a little, allowing him room to think of more questions. He voiced none of them, but she seemed to see them in his eyes.

"I will not tell you your name; not yet, nor why you are my prisoner. I will not promise you freedom, Mirror. And I will not promise you death." She wasn't looking at him anymore; her gaze was focused inward, as if she saw someone else entirely. "You will remain my prisoner, and you will do my bidding."

In perfect honesty, he said, "I would not have it any other way." And watched her try to search his gaze for deceit; watched her try to find a hint of lie in his statement. And watched her fail. She stared at him. He found enough courage to stare back.

"You would be content as my prisoner?" she finally asked, her voice disbelieving. "Not knowing your name or your past? Content to do my bidding until I tire of you? And what then? What if I locked you away in an attic, and forgot you ever existed?"

"That is your right," he whispered, answering her last question first. "I serve you. You are my Queen." And, greatly daring, "I think... I think I would rather not know." When he finally glanced back up at her, he saw she looked stricken, as if she couldn't quite believe his words. As if she couldn't quite believe what he had said.

She pulled a strand of beads from around her neck. They glinted softly in the lamplight, a riot of blues and greens and purples, a rainbow cupped in her hands.

"These beads will protect you from Terrin's spells," she said gruffly, and poured them into his hands. *He felt her touch as he could feel nothing else.* The beads did not fade to gray as he clutched them, but remained vibrant and pure, a piece of her magic...a piece of her self. As she bent over him, something rustled in her dress, and her hands flew to her pockets. She pulled out a grubby piece of paper, stared at it for a moment, and cursed.

"Teluride."

"If I can help the Prince..." the Ghost began, struggling up.

Skade turned away from him. "I will not risk your life so soon," she replied. "I can do this myself, although it would be easier using the mirror..."

"My Queen." His voice was soft, but insistent. She turned. "Please. Let me help." He managed to prop himself up on one arm, gasping a little at the residual pain. "Please."

She stared at him for a long while, her eyes and face showing no emotion; no sign of what she would reply. Finally, she sighed, and raised one hand. A new mirror appeared on the wall, spanning floor to ceiling, less ornate than the first, but nearly twice as big. It shimmered slightly, and he saw his reflection in a mirror for the first time. *He saw himself.*

His entire form was gray, an insubstantial form that blended in with the bloody quilts so well he almost couldn't see where they ended and his body began. He was young; younger than Skade in appearance, at least, for he had no true realization of how old his Queen actually was. His hair, though gray, was cut short and unevenly, as if he had done it himself before he became her prisoner. His clothing was no longer torn to shreds.

And there was no blood. He glanced down at himself, just to make sure, and found the mirror's reflection to be truth. The blood on the quilts was still there, but his skin no longer seeped; the wounds were no longer evident. He still felt weak, but he thought he could do her bidding; serve his Queen, one last time before his strength gave out.

Skade sighed, then gave him a small smile. "Remember what I told you," she said. "Wear the beads. And make your prison what you expect it to be like."

"Yes, My Lady."

"I will allow you to walk to the mirror if you wish."

He could already feel the spell tugging him into the mirror, but he no longer truly minded the journey. He slowly got to his feet, swaying a little, then walked into the mirror of his own volition.

Not one thought of escape or flight ever crossed into his waking mind.

Chapter 11

Alban almost made it to Teluride's room. He stumbled on the stairs and would have fallen, but Kyne caught his arm and held him until he managed to regain his footing.

"You should be in bed," she whispered, "not sneaking around this castle. What am I supposed to do if you aren't strong enough to follow me out of here? I can't carry both you and Teluride."

"I told you what to do if my father catches me again," Alban whispered, wanting only to curl up and sleep. He rubbed his eyes and tried to focus, but it was like wading through quicksand. "We have to hurry. He'll be here soon."

"How soon?" Kyne pulled him up the last set of stairs, and he collapsed against the wall.

"I don't know." He couldn't seem to catch his breath, and he was afraid that the spots of gray at the edges of his vision would only grow worse.

"And what will we do if Teluride's under a spell?" Kyne's voice broke through his weariness and forced him upright again. "You hardly have enough strength to stand. And I don't have the right training for breaking spells."

"I don't know." The look he gave her was bleak and hopeless, almost as if he expected to fail. He pushed away from the wall and continued down the hall. "But we have to try."

He almost didn't want to open the door when they reached it. There were no guards. At this hour everyone seemed to be asleep and he wished he could join them. The door opened before he could try, and he stepped back, expecting Terrin, somehow, but the vampire motioned them inside.

"How do you feel?" Kyne whispered as she passed.

The vampire hesitated. "I haven't truly fed. I want to be away from here before Terrin returns." He turned away before she could reply. "Teluride is awake, but I don't think he can walk very far." He paused. "And he remembers nothing."

"That would be best, considering what crime Terrin claims he has committed..." Something in the vampire's voice made Kyne pause. "*Nothing?*"

"I had to tell him his name."

Alban sank down on the foot of Teluride's bed, his head in his hands. The Prince stirred at his approach, and opened his eyes, but it was very obvious he recognized no one but the vampire. It was also very obvious that he wouldn't be able to walk anywhere.

"Did you bring him any food?" the vampire asked. "I don't think Terrin bothered to feed him..."

"All I have is what Alban didn't eat of the broth," Kyne replied, and held up a small skin. "It isn't much. We didn't have enough time to stop by the kitchen." She glanced at the closed door. "And I have no idea how much time we'll have here." She glanced at Alban and frowned. "I am no wizard, and Alban is too exhausted to manage a portal. Have you thought at all how we're going to get out of here?"

"I've been too busy trying to stay alive," the vampire whispered.

"You will accept the offer my Queen has to give you," a new voice whispered from the darkness. Both Kyne and the vampire turned to face it. Alban paid it no mind, and Teluride closed his eyes.

"You!" The vampire sounded surprised. "I thought you said you wouldn't be coming back."

The Ghost shrugged. "I go where I am bid to go," he whispered. "Will you accept my Queen's offer?"

"It depends on what her offer is." This from Alban, who looked almost awake.

"Your freedom." The Ghost's voice was mild. "She will open a portal to this room, and all of you can join her in Iomar."

"And what will she want from us in return?" Alban's eyes glittered, almost as if he was holding back tears.

"Your unending loyalty and your firstborn son. What do you think?" Teluride had a mirror across from his bed and the most beautiful woman Alban had ever seen appeared in it, looking a little annoyed. Her flame red hair seemed to light up the room, shoving shadows away. "I came here to help you, nothing more. If you don't need my help, then my Mirror and I will depart."

Alban looked like he wanted to argue with her, but Kyne smoothly stepped in. "We need your help. And my Queen will appreciate this, I'm sure."

"You can visit with your sister while you are here," Skade replied, and smiled at the look on Kyne's face.

"Eadda?"

"The very same. I rescued her after Terrin's Hounds decided to defend his little secret." She did something with her hands, and the mirror seemed to shimmer. "Alban!" Her voice brought his head up again. "Do you know anything of your father's Dreamer?"

Alban stared at her. "I..." He shook his head. "Dreamer?"

"I do," the vampire said softly.

Skade glanced at him. "Then we will have to talk a bit when you are safe and warm and...well-fed." The vampire looked at her in surprise. "Step through the mirror, and you will be with me. Kyne, can you carry Teluride?"

"How is it that he wasn't protected by any spells?" Kyne asked. "I expected Terrin to..."

Skade stared at the Ghost. "My Mirror...took care of the spells," she said. "He *was* well-guarded." Mistress and Ghost stared at each other for a minute longer, then Skade stepped back from the mirror. "Kyne, you first, with Teluride. I think it will be best for him to see my healers as soon as possible." She looked around at them again, her gaze stopping on Alban. "And then the rest of you, of course."

Kyne carefully lifted Teluride, who didn't make a sound. "You'll be safe soon," she whispered, and he managed a smile. When she stepped through the mirror, the Ghost's form shivered and faded, nearly vanishing at one point. Skade looked at him oddly, but made no comment.

"Alban, you're next."

He could see people moving behind her now, another red-haired woman taking Teluride from Kyne's arms and bearing him away. He managed to stand, holding onto the bed for support.

"Everything I've ever known has been a lie," he whispered, staring at Skade, his eyes fever-bright.

"Not your friendship with Teluride," Skade replied. "Not the fact that you are a wizard."

"How do I know I can trust you?" He stopped a few feet away from the mirror. "How do I know you won't turn me over to my father?"

"Alban!" The vampire sounded shocked that he would even think of such a thing.

But instead of getting angry, Skade merely smiled. "I commend you on your caution, Alban," she said, and held out her hand to him, pushing through the mirror. "And I'm sorry I cannot give you more peace of mind. You can only have my word. If that isn't good enough, then I don't know what to tell you." She sounded perfectly serious.

Alban stared at her for a moment longer, then took her hand. He stumbled as she drew him through the mirror, and by the time he stood on the other side, consciousness was quickly replaced by drowning both sight and sound in a cacophony of darkness. He fell to his knees.

Skade turned away from him and faced the vampire, who now hesitated in the shadows, the only one left in the room. Even the Ghost was gone.

"Come with me," she said, and offered him her hand. "No one will harm you here."

He drew back, pressed against the bed, his hood hiding the look on his face. "But I will have to harm someone if I go with you, my Lady. I haven't truly eaten in over a month. Even now..." drew a deep, shaky breath. "I don't know if I can..."

"You must call me Skade." She stepped out of the mirror and smoothed her blue dress down over her hips. "Let me see your face, vampire. I like to see who I am speaking to."

Even then, he hesitated, then one white hand reached up to remove his hood. His face was pale and cadaverously thin, his blue eyes huge and ringed with shadows. Lank black hair fell across those eyes, and he pushed it away.

Skade fingered the strands of beads around her neck as she stared at him, then she held out her hand again. "Come with me to Iomar. I swear to you that you will be safe."

"But..."

"And I want to know about Terrin's Dreamer."

"But..." He seemed at loss for words.

"Come with me." Her eyes seemed to glow suddenly, and he had to force himself not to back away. "Come with me, and we'll figure out some way to feed you. I might not approve of vampires," and here she smiled, "but that doesn't mean you will starve in my care."

"It would be nice to be away from Terrin," the vampire said carefully, his eyes fastened on her face. He seemed to want her to leave him, or forbid him to come. He seemed to expect it, and Skade wasn't about to give him the pleasure. And she was getting tired of holding out her hand. As far as she knew, Terrin could return any minute now, and the ruse would be up.

"You don't want to annoy me," she said after a moment, still staring at him. "Surely you've heard of me if you've been around long enough. I do not break my word, and I have given it to you."

"You bend your word sometimes," the vampire murmured.

Skade rolled her eyes, refusing to get angry with him. And she'd thought *Alban* was paranoid.

"How many times do I have to swear?" she asked, her patience finally giving out. The vampire stared at her for a moment more, then smiled. The smile never reached his eyes.

"I've also heard that you aren't very patient," he whispered, and stepped forward. "I'll come with you, Skade." His hand was shockingly cold in her grasp, but she showed no sign of pulling away. Instead, she pulled him into the mirror, away from Leysan and into the fabled Island Kingdom of Iomar.

Safe. But for how long?

Zaira awoke and for one short moment, could not remember what had happened or why she hurt so much. She lay still in the bed for a little while, trying to hear if her father watched again from the doorway, but she heard only dripping water, and smelled only blood and rain.

She opened her eyes. Her eyelashes wanted to stick together, but she managed to pry them apart without much trouble, and the pain from that was nothing compared to her bruises and cuts. She managed to sit up, and sat on the edge of the bloody sheets for a while, head bowed low over her legs, fighting nausea and the blackness that wanted to claim her. Would she be able to survive daily beatings until Skade came, or would Skade arrive to find her a mindless husk, a dead thing fit only for burial?

She pushed her mind away from such thoughts and tried to stand. Her legs buckled under her weight. There was blood on the floor here, too, she saw, and her father's dagger, its hilt covered with blood, halfway under the bed. She touched the tip of the sheathed weapon, and wondered if she had enough strength to use it to protect herself. Or enough courage.

Or, if things got too bad for her, and Skade didn't come, would she use it on herself?

She pushed the dagger farther under the bed, and managed to get to her knees. Even that small movement cost her dearly.

The window leaked freely, and the gray day outside showed no sign of letting in any sunlight. Zaira slowly crawled towards the puddle of water on the floor, and stared down at her bloody reflection. She knew the water wasn't clean, but she had spent the last six years drinking rainwater, and she had not died. She scooped up some in her hands and sipped. Even the water tasted of blood, but it cleared the blockage in her throat. She leaned her aching head against the cool wall, and tried not to think of what would happen next.

She was so tired.

Zaira almost fell asleep right there, which would have been a mistake since she was well in view of anyone peeking through the door. Only a little strengthened by the water, she got to her knees again and crawled back to the bed. There was no place to hide in the room, and she could not climb the wall and escape out the window. She would be trapped until Skade came for her, and even then, she wasn't certain she would still be alive.

She felt tears prick at the corners of her eyes, stinging both bruises and cuts as they made their way down her face. She hadn't allowed herself to cry in six years, knowing tears would be just as futile as escape. But here, in the castle she would have been living in if she were still alive...here, she could cry, for she did not know if her dreams would come true. Here, not knowing when her father would next visit; not knowing if Terrin would have enough strength to return and punish her for not telling him the whole truth... Here she could cry, for she did not know how long she would live.

Chapter 12

Chaos reigned for a little while, especially when Alban collapsed across Skade's thick rugs and could not be awakened. Teluride and Alban soon lay in the care of the healers; Kyne went off in search of her sister, and the vampire stayed on the floor where he'd ended up, head bowed inside the hood, trying to find the strength to pay attention to the riches around him.

Now that he was safe, all he wanted to do was fall asleep, but the hunger battling down his defenses would never let him sleep. He dully wondered if Skade knew that, and decided he didn't really care. He was alone in her rooms for the time being, save for the Ghost in the mirror, who had vanished a little while ago. Teluride, Alban, and Kyne were gone, presumably to rest and be healed. But what would it take for him to heal? Would he be forced to murder one of Skade's servants to regain a fraction of his strength?

The door opened, but he didn't have enough strength to raise his head. All of his strength was bent on forcing the hunger back; forcing it to behave and not break free to devour whoever was unlucky enough to be in his way.

Then, suddenly, Skade knelt in front of him, holding out a cup full of blood so fresh it steamed. He stared at her, eyes dulled by hunger.

"I will not murder someone for my own gain." His voice cracked.

Skade smiled, genuinely amused. "Do you think I'd let one of my servants die for you?" she asked. "The person who donated this blood is resting with a mug of nourishing tea. She didn't die, and I do not wish you to." She offered him the cup. "Please drink. If you need more, I can get more."

He took the cup and stared at it for a moment, as if he'd forgotten how to drink. It had been so long... But with the first sip he found he could not stop, and the cup was empty before he blinked.

"I'll get more."

He managed to push the hunger away enough to shake his head. "If I drink too much at once, I might..."

"But if you don't drink more, you won't heal."

He sighed. "True." He was almost too tired to speak.

"So you'll let me bring you more?" Skade stood, forcing him to look up at her. "Are you comfortable enough here?"

"I would be comfortable anywhere, my Lady," the vampire whispered.

"If you are to be my guest, you should call me Skade."

He was too exhausted to reply to that.

When Terrin reached Leysan, he knew he was too late. Of course, no one in the castle had seen what had happened, and there had been no earthly guard on Teluride's door. He wasted precious moments arguing with the Council, who professed they knew nothing about the Prince's escape, and wasted even more time with the palace guard, ordering them out into the forest to search, even though he already knew Teluride escaped by magic.

It didn't occur to him to see to Alban until nearly dawn, and when he found Alban's door wide open, and both his son, the assassin and the vampire gone, he thought he had a pretty good idea who had stolen them. Who but Cynara would dare to go so far to rescue one of her own?

But they had left by a mirror; of that much he was certain. It bore a taint of unfamiliar magic, and as far as Terrin knew, Cynara didn't use mirror magic. Who, then, had taken them? What friends had Alban made, and how? He scowled at Teluride's mirror, and resolved to return to Glinyeu and Zaira as soon as he was able. With Alban gone, his recovery from the spells' destruction would be slower, but he would be in Glinyeu by the end of two days. He thought he could manage that. Zaira had lied to him for the last time.

Mirror magic. What damn witch in all of Cruinne used mirror magic?

And then he knew, as easily as that. He knew both the reason he could not track them...they had fled over water, and who had helped them...Skade.

And he had to wonder if he'd get to Glinyeu before she stole his Dreamer out from under his nose, as well.

Alban opened his eyes to a flurry of activity around him. He almost let them slide shut again, but the red-haired woman bending over him favored him with such a kind smile that he couldn't find the heart to retreat into darkness again.

"You're awake." She sounded surprised, as if she hadn't expected him to wake up at all. "How do you feel?"

Alban considered that question very carefully. His body still ached, but it was a healing ache now, and the gnawing hunger had been sated. "Better." His voice cracked. "Where is..." For a moment he couldn't remember who had saved him. "Skade?"

"She just left," the woman whispered. "I think she wanted to go visit Prince Teluride. Do you want me to find her for you?"

"No, don't bother her," Alban said quickly. He thought about sitting up, and decided against it when the smallest of movements had the room swaying around his head. "The others?"

"The Lady Kyne is still here," the woman said. "And the Nameless One has not ventured from Skade's chambers."

The Nameless One had to be the vampire. Relief washed over him in a wave. "How long have I been asleep?" he asked.

"A day, no more," the woman replied, "and you should sleep again, Alban. You need to regain your strength."

Weariness dragged him down until he thought he would surrender to the darkness again, but he pushed it back. "Tell Skade..."

When he didn't continue, the woman smoothed clean hair over his brow. "What would you like me to tell her?" she asked.

"Tell her, thank you," Alban whispered, and closed his eyes.

This time, he slept for two days.

"I think we need to talk."

The vampire had not ventured outside of Skade's room since she'd brought him through the mirror. He had no idea if Alban or Teluride were still alive; he'd only seen Skade twice since then.

She had been unusually patient, from what he remembered hearing about her. She hadn't demanded answers right away, only sent an endless stream of servants with what seemed to be an endless stream of blood.

He could feel his body healing for the first time he remembered. His eyesight sharpened, his skin no longer felt so cold. He knew he should be happy he was alive.

Why, then, did he feel so guilty?

"About?" His voice was the only thing that hadn't recovered.

"Terrin's Dreamer." Skade, resplendent in another vivid blue gown, leaned against her door and smiled at him.

The vampire hadn't quite managed to bring himself to sleep in her bed. He had no idea where she slept. He hadn't quite managed to shed the cloak, either; it had kept him safe for so long that he felt naked without it.

"What do you want to know?"

"That all depends on how much *you* know," Skade replied. "Have you taken a bath since you got here?"

"N-no." It had been so long since he had been clean that he hadn't really thought about it.

"Then a bath first," Skade decided. "Can you walk?"

He had yet to try. "I don't know."

Skade stepped into the room and shut the door behind her. "It won't be far; I have a private bath." She vanished through a doorway the vampire hadn't really noticed, and soon steam billowed out, slightly scented with lavender. When Skade reappeared, the water droplets in her red hair shone like jewels.

"I'll...ah...have someone clean your cloak."

He stood, holding onto her bed for support, wondering how he'd managed before with hardly any blood to drink. He couldn't remember much about the last month or so; the memories seemed to have been buried, and he was content to leave them buried.

When he shed his cloak, he blinked a little in the torchlight, unused to having light full on his face. It had been easier, in Leysan, to wear it all the time; any stray ray of sunlight could kill him as easily as Alban's spell had been killing him.

His body felt strange without the cloak. Lighter, perhaps, but vulnerable, although he knew his cloak did not have any magical properties.

Skade regarded him from the bathroom door, her arms folded. "How old were you when Terrin had you made into a vampire?" she asked.

The vampire shied away from the question, not wanting to probe too deeply when he felt so strange. "I don't know."

Skade's eyes narrowed. For a moment, he feared he had angered her, and she would send him back to Terrin. He froze.

"I think you do know, but I can understand if you don't wish to remember," she said. "Your bath awaits. Take as long as you like; I'll be right outside the door if you need any help."

The vampire stepped inside the room, and closed the door behind him.

It took him a while to remember how to remove his clothes, and he studiously ignored the fogged up mirror when he slipped into the hot water.

And for the first time in many years, he allowed his body to relax enough to enjoy the sensation of being clean.

An hour passed, maybe two. The water did not cool off, as it would have in any other tub; evidently Skade turned her magic to mundane matters as well as rescuing complete strangers from castles halfway across the world.

The vampire scrubbed until he could scrub no more, washing years of dirt and filth and fear from his body as well as his mind. He thought he might have to change the water, but it remained clear, save for the poultices of herbs floating through it. He crushed one of the bags, and inhaled the scent of mint, closing his eyes to savor the feeling of utter safety.

He didn't know how to feel safe. Perhaps that was part of his problem, he sensed; he could not ever remember being safe before.

When the temperature of the water abruptly cooled, he climbed out and reached for a towel. Only then did he realize he had no other clothes than the ones he'd been wearing for so long, and he was curiously reluctant to put them on again.

"If you're quite finished, I have some clothes you might want to try on," Skade said from the other side of the door. "I'll put them on the floor, and I promise I won't look."

The vampire almost smiled. He waited for a moment, then opened the door.

"Try them on," Skade said from the other side of the room. She had her back to him, and her red hair curled down past her beaded belt. The vampire tore his eyes away from her, and gathered up the clothes. "We can find you a pair of shoes after we talk; I wasn't certain what size you would wear."

Without speaking, he retreated back into the bathroom and closed the door. The clothes were fine...finer than he had ever seen, and his fingers fumbled on the buttons as he pulled them on.

Everything fit perfectly, from the dusty black shirt to the heavy socks, to the pants that felt like butter against his skin. Quite suddenly, his eyes filled with tears, and he sank down against the side of the bathtub, unable to face Skade and tell her what she wanted to know.

The bathroom door opened.

The vampire wiped his face and started to rise, stumbling a little in his haste.

"Don't be afraid of me," Skade said from the doorway, her gaze a mixture of emotions too complex for the vampire to sort out. "I swear to you..."

"I know." His voice cracked. "No one will harm me here. That's not the problem." He ran one hand through his wet hair, and sat on the edge of the tub. Skade walked into the room and carefully put one hand on his shoulder. He had to steel himself not to pull away.

"I understand," she whispered, her voice uncommonly gentle. "Do you want to talk about it?"

The vampire sighed. "I would rather forget, my Lady," he said honestly. "There isn't much I want to remember." He paused. "I've never been safe before."

"I'll do my best to make sure you are safe from now on," Skade said. "Shall we go?" She held out her hand, and he took it, noticing for the first time that his skin was no longer the dead white of a corpse. His veins ran with stolen blood, both healing and warming him.

His eyes filled with tears again, but he blinked them away, not wanting Skade to see.

She did not comment on his tears, but led him to a small tea table, which had been set up at one end of the room. It held a delicate china teapot, a single teacup already full of steaming tea, and what was beginning to be a familiar set of earthenware mugs.

"Now, we'll talk," Skade said, and helped him sit.

"What would you like to know?" He could only hope the telling didn't hurt as much as living through the memories had. But the bath and the endless supply of blood had washed away the fog from his mind, and he realized as he pulled his chair up to the table that he would willingly tell Skade anything, just as long as he did not have to return to Leysan ever again.

Chapter 13

For two days, Eabon left Zaira alone, and Zaira almost dared to hope that she had been forgotten. She spent her days lying on the bloody bed, staring at the path the sunlight made across the cracked ceiling, waiting for rescue, or death.

Sometimes she thought even death would be better than rescue, for she would escape from the dreams if she died. But then she remembered Skade's grand castle, and the servants, and the food, and knew she did not want to die forgotten and buried in an unmarked grave of Terrin's choosing.

She wanted to die free.

On the third day, Zaira heard Eabon stumbling down the hall, long before he reached his room. She started from the bed, unaccustomed movement sending the room spinning around her head, and frantically searched for a place to hide. Her body--especially her face--was still swollen and sore from the beating, and she did not want to endure that again.

For some reason, her eyes were drawn to the window high up in the wall. Zaira froze, staring at it, her mind awash with new possibilities now; the slim possibility that she might be able to escape.

Terrin would take days to return. Even though the course of events showed Zaira that she might not die by her father's hands, she had no desire to be beaten again.

She had the bed, which was almost tall enough for her to reach the windowsill if she stood on tiptoes. She had her father's dagger, which could be used to break the loose glass, the wind rattling through the window and the leak that supplied her with water attested that it was not strong in its casing.

Zaira held her breath and tested the possibilities in her mind. *Could she escape?* Would her escape--provided she actually managed to climb out the narrow window--change some part of the future that should not be changed?

Selfishly, Zaira decided she didn't care.

It took most of her strength to drag the heavy metal bed over to the window, and even more to break the ancient pane of glass with the dagger. She almost forgot to look down when the glass shattered, and thought it would be ironic if Terrin's Dreamer blinded herself out of sheer stupidity.

She didn't bother to shake the glass out of her hair, but used the dagger to knock the rest of the glass out of the frame.

Now came the hardest part, getting through the window.

Something clattered in the corridor outside. Zaira jumped and almost dropped the dagger. She clearly heard her father curse, mumble something, and shuffle farther down the corridor, not stopping at her door.

Her heartbeat sounded too loud in her ears. Zaira's vision flickered, and the room spun a slow spiral around her head. She swayed on the bed and almost fell.

If she planned to escape, she would have to do it now, before Eabon returned, and she was too weak to try. She took a deep breath and reached up for the edge of the windowsill, almost drawing back when the shards of glass still left in the casing cut her hands. She threw the dagger out ahead of her, grabbed the sides of the window, and kicked off from the bed, bare toes scrabbling for purchase on the pitted stone wall.

Glass sliced into moon-pale skin as she scrambled up, but Zaira resolutely told herself she didn't care. She felt the tender skin of her feet split under unaccustomed pressure, and the stone became slick with her blood.

An hour later, panting and dazed, barely able to see in the watery sunlight, Zaira lay outside in the dead grass, and realized that she faced the woods. There were no gawking peasants to worry about; there were no other signs of life at all, save for the castle at her back, rising far up over her head. She realized she'd been at the bottom of one of the towers, and hoped her father didn't have guards posted in the top who would see her and sound the alarm.

She wiped bloody hands in the wet grass, picked a piece of glass out of her palm, and gathered up the dagger. Then, limping, leaving a trail of blood in the grass that any idiot could follow, Zaira staggered into the woods.

She was another hour away from the castle, and deep into the thickest part of the forest, before she allowed herself to collapse.

Alban awoke slowly, reveling in the strange sensation that he was in a bed; warm, clean, and comfortable for the first time in months. He opened his eyes, and found he lay in the same bed as before, but there were no red-haired women bending over him this time.

Indeed, the room was hushed with the silence that only appeared very early in the morning, that special silence that told him most of the castle lay in dreams around him.

He sat up, half-expecting the room to swing around his head, but the walls stayed in place, and he felt clear-headed for the first time since he had awakened and realized his father had put him under a spell. Before he realized he'd decided to stand, he'd slid his legs out from under the blankets and settled bare feet on the cold stone floor.

"I'm not quite sure you should get up yet," Skade stepped out of the shadows, and Alban jumped, wondering how he had missed her before.

The Queen of Iomar's favorite color had to be blue, unless she merely had a fondness for the vivid color of the summer sky. It suited her; the red hair curling down past her waist seemed brighter because of it. But, Alban reflected, Skade would be beautiful in dull blacks and grays.

"You've been asleep for two days," she said, before he could ask. "More recovery than anything else, I think; Kyne has told me as much as she knows about the spell." She smiled. "Teluride has been asleep on and off since Kyne carried him through. I just got finished talking to the vampire, and you were the only one left."

"How did you know I would wake up?" Alban asked.

Skade shrugged. "If you weren't awake, I would have gone to bed myself. I can't remember the last time I had a full night's sleep."

"If I'm keeping you up..." Alban began.

"I don't need much sleep," Skade said. "Do you remember what happened, or should I bring you up to date?"

"I remember." Alban would rather *not* remember, but he couldn't seem to block out anything but the past month, under the spell. Those memories were thankfully still buried. "What are you going to do with us now?" He was very aware that he was, in effect, Skade's prisoner.

"Not my prisoner," Skade said softly. "I don't ever treat my prisoners this well."

"Then what?" Alban asked, a little discomforted that she seemed to be reading his mind.

"I'm not reading your mind, by the way," she said, on the tail end of that thought. "I can see the questions in your eyes, Alban. You have very expressive eyes."

He dropped his gaze. "What are you going to do?"

Skade sighed. "Look at me, Alban."

He had to force himself to obey.

"Why are you so afraid of me?" Skade slowly walked over to his bed, and sat down on a wooden chair. "What have I ever done to you?"

"I'm not afraid of you," Alban said, but he knew she knew he was lying. "I'm..." he stopped, frustrated when the words would not come, "Kyne said I am a wizard."

"You are." Skade twisted a multi-colored strand of her beads around one finger. "Untrained, but that doesn't mean you cannot be trained."

"I don't know if I *want* to be a wizard," Alban said miserably, remembering the horrible draining of his father's spell.

"Unfortunately, you don't have much choice in that matter," Skade said. "Wizards and witches never get a choice. We are born the way we are."

Alban's vision blurred, and he blinked the tears away. "I hurt the vampire," he whispered.

"I know you did," Skade said, her voice soft. "And you hurt Kyne too, but she'll get over it. That was more hurt pride than anything, I think."

"But if I wasn't a wizard, I wouldn't have been able to hurt them!" Alban cried.

"There is that," Skade agreed. "But that is also in the past. You can't change anything now; you can only train your powers so your father won't be able to trap you again so easily."

Alban contemplated being trapped under that spell again, and shivered. "Are you going to let us stay here?" he asked.

"Not Teluride. He's too badly injured for my healers to handle. I don't like it that he's lost his memory; without it, he may never find out what happened to his father."

"Where will he go?" Alban asked, and wondered if he knew anything about King Valdis's death. Valdis had been like a father to him in the years Terrin was gone, and now he was dead. This time, he couldn't stop the tears.

Skade waited until he had dried his eyes before continuing. "I have a call out to an associate of mine," she said. "If Espen can't help Teluride, no one in Cruinne can."

"Espen?" Alban couldn't imagine why that name would sound so familiar.

"You might have met her once," Skade said. "But she left Cruinne soon after your father came back."

Left Cruinne? How could someone leave a whole world? Alban decided not to ask. "So what happens now?" He asked. "None of us can go back to Leysan..."

"I'd hope none of you want to go back to Leysan," Skade said dryly. "I don't know, Alban, why don't you tell me what you want to do?" She stared at him critically for a moment. "How old are you, anyway?"

"F-Fifteen," Alban whispered. "What *I* want to do?"

"Yes." Skade's face showed nothing but polite interest. "Would you like to train your powers here in Iomar?"

Alban blinked. "I..." He didn't quite know what to say. "I'd like to," he finally whispered, confused that she would leave that decision up to him. "But what about my father?"

"Leave Terrin to me and the rest of the Council of Kingdoms," Skade said cryptically. "I doubt he'll get very far in his plans if both you and his Dreamer are gone."

"You have his Dreamer?" Alban asked, although he had no real idea what the Dreamer actually was.

Skade frowned. "Not yet," she admitted, "but it's only a matter of time. I'm planning to go to Glinyeu tomorrow and rescue her." She stared at Alban intently. "Would you like to come with me? I can swear that you'll be perfectly safe."

Alban's breath caught in his throat. "I..."

Skade patted his shoulder, and he was too dazed to flinch away. "Sleep on it," she said. "I'll send a servant round in the morning for your answer."

Before Alban could reply, she was gone in a flutter of red hair and blue gown, leaving him dazed and confused as to why she had invited him along.

Did she think he would *want* to go to Glinyeu? He didn't even know what his father's Dreamer *was*. He fell asleep an hour later, still mulling over his silent protests.

Alban dreamed that night of the lonely tower he had so briefly seen in Leysan, and the small white hand of the person walled up inside.

Chapter 14

Early the next morning, Skade slipped into her room, leaving the lights off so the vampire didn't wake up. She stepped up to the Mirror and folded her arms.

"Show me Zaira."

The Ghost appeared. She could tell he had recovered; the pinched look on his face had vanished, but he had lost most of his previous fear of her, too.

She wasn't quite sure if she liked that.

"Terrin's Dreamer?" The Ghost spoke in a whisper, too, staring over her shoulder at the vampire, who had finally been persuaded to sleep in her bed. Skade was a little surprised he had slept through her arrival. He must have been more exhausted than she thought.

"Eabon's daughter," Skade said. "She's in Glinyeu; you can find her there, can't you?"

"If there's a mirror or a puddle of water, I can find her," the Ghost said, and vanished.

Minutes passed. Skade leaned against the wall and watched the vampire sleep. He looked so young asleep--no more than twelve and no less than ten, she thought. That Terrin would do something so...permanent to a child infuriated her.

"My Queen?" The fear was back in the Ghost's voice. Skade turned.

"Did you find her?" she asked.

"Not exactly..."

"Not exactly?" She did, perhaps, owe him something for probably saving Teluride's life, so she steeled her voice not to be annoyed.

"She's gone." The Ghost faded before she could reply to that, and a small room appeared in the Mirror by way of a puddle of water on the floor.

A narrow bed had been dragged across the floor to sit under a tiny window, and by the streaks of blood on the wall, Skade could very well guess what had happened.

"She escaped?"

"It looks that way, my Lady."

There was blood on the bed, too, and dried streaks of it on the floor where the bed had been.

As she watched, the barred door slammed open, and the mad king Eabon staggered inside. For a moment, he did not seem to realize what had happened, but the glass on the bloody sheets soon sent him reeling out of the room again, his face white with fear.

Fear? Why would he be afraid that Zaira had escaped? And where was he now?

"Can you find her?" Skade asked. Alban would be happy that he didn't have to make a decision; she'd seen his reluctance quite clearly when she suggested he go to Glinyeu with her.

"I'm not sure," the Ghost replied, letting the horrible little room fade away. "I might be able to if I knew what to look for, but..."

Skade sighed. "But no one knows what Zaira looks like."

"I do," the vampire said from behind them. Skade turned. Awake, he seemed much older, and he carried himself as if the weight of his memories were a heavy burden on his thin shoulders. Skade supposed they must be, if he was as old as she thought he was.

"You've seen Zaira?" she asked.

The vampire nodded. "After Terrin's potions changed her."

"You didn't tell me about this last night," Skade said softly.

The vampire flinched. "I thought you knew," he said. "You seemed to know so much about her..."

"I read her diary," Skade said, remembering the crabbed writing in the dusty book. "But even Zaira didn't know *everything*."

"Yes, she does," the vampire said, and shivered.

"Forgive me if I don't believe you," Skade said. "She didn't know she was going to escape from Glinyeu."

"She escaped?" An emotion Skade could not decipher flitted across the vampire's face. "Good."

"Tell me what Terrin did to Zaira," Skade instructed. "Or would you rather show me? The Mirror can show what you're describing."

The vampire hesitated. For a moment, Skade thought he wouldn't allow her into his mind like that, but then he steeled himself and slowly nodded.

"All you have to do is hold the scene in your head and touch the mirror," Skade explained. "I won't be able to see anything but what you show me, and you can break contact with the mirror whenever you want."

The vampire slid off the bed and slowly approached the blank mirror, then placed one hand on the mirror's cold, slick surface. Skade's reflection shivered.

"Sit down," Skade said softly, and made a chair appear behind the vampire. He sat. "Now show me what Terrin did to Zaira."

For a moment, the mirror remained blank, then as Skade watched, her reflection faded and vanished, leaving darkness behind. The darkness slowly formed to become a corridor, presumably in Glinyeu's now-destroyed castle.

"She's been very sick, my Lord."

Skade would have recognized Terrin's voice anywhere. She saw a white hand touch the smooth stone of the corridor, and then Terrin himself, standing with Eabon outside an unremarkable wooden door.

Eabon glanced the vampire's way and stiffened. "I want to see my daughter," he insisted. "You said she was getting well yesterday, Terrin! I haven't seen her for two weeks!"

"Very well," Terrin sighed, but Skade sensed something else in his voice; something...almost expectant, as if he *wanted* Eabon's reaction to what his daughter had become.

Terrin opened the door, and Eabon walked inside. The vampire followed, keeping to the shadows.

"Can't you light a lamp?" Skade heard Eabon say, and then the vampire was in the room, hiding in the darkness in the corner, in full sight of the bed.

From the vampire's point of view, the room was only a little dim, not nearly as black as it would have been to Eabon.

"The light hurts her eyes," she heard Terrin say, as she stared at the small figure lying asleep in a bed far too large for her.

Eabon turned up the lamp anyway, and Skade stared in horror at what the Princess of Glinyeu had become.

"Zaira had always been small," the vampire whispered, his eyes closed. "But her hair was jet black, like her father's, and her eyes were green."

The girl on the bed had hair the color of milk. Her skin was just as pale, almost blending in with the white sheets. Her eyes were closed, her breathing labored.

"What did Terrin *do*?" Skade breathed, horrified.

"Zaira had a talent," the vampire whispered. "Terrin tried to harness that talent and make it stronger when Zaira got sick."

"Did it work?" this from the Ghost, who sounded sickened.

"To a degree," the vampire said. "Zaira must answer any question put to her--so therefore, she knows the future as soon as you ask her a question."

"How old is she here?" Skade asked, trying to remember what year Zaira had supposedly died.

"Six," the vampire whispered.

Skade tried to imagine a six-year-old locked up in a lonely tower, and wondered how Zaira could still be sane. She had no doubt she was; her diary had attested to that. But where was she now?

The scene in the mirror faded, and the ghost took its place as the vampire sat back.

"Can you find her?" Skade asked.

The Ghost nodded. "It might take me a day or two, but I can find her."

"Then do so." Skade turned away from the mirror and stared blindly at her room. "If I had known..."

"You didn't," the vampire whispered, "and the past cannot be changed."

"How true." Skade sighed. "I suppose I should go tell Alban he doesn't have to go to Glinyeu with me, after all."

"I hope your Ghost can find him," the vampire said softly. "I liked Zaira." He stopped, as if not wanting to go any farther, and Skade watched him almost physically retreat from the question of Zaira. She wondered what else he hadn't told her about Terrin's Dreamer, then decided not to press.

"Perhaps, since you knew her, you'd like to come with me," Skade suggested. "Alban didn't seem very pleased with the prospect of a journey."

"Alban..." the vampire hesitated, "I don't think Alban will want to go anywhere for a long time."

"He might not have a choice," Skade pointed out.

"He's not a bad person," the vampire said softly.

"I know he's not." Skade looked at him and waited, but he didn't seem to want to go on. "He must have hurt you very badly." The night before, they had spoken about trivial things, more to put him at ease than anything else. She still hadn't uncovered the exact nature of Alban's spell.

The vampire's fingers twitched, as if he wished for the shelter of his cloak. "Nothing Terrin had ever done to me could compare to Alban's spell," he finally whispered, and Skade thought she saw tears in his eyes.

"What did he do?" Skade asked gently.

The vampire turned away. "It might be better if you didn't know," he finally said.

Skade didn't reply. After a moment, he sighed and shook his head.

"Terrin has done horrible things to me over the years, but never something that would kill me," he whispered, and gave her a twisted smile. "I can only drink human blood. Everything else is poison to me." He paused. "Alban took that away."

"He did *what?*" Skade asked, aghast.

"I felt myself dying for the month he was under the spell," the vampire whispered. "I had to drink blood, I'd die if I didn't."

"But when you drank it..."

"It burned my mouth like poison," the vampire whispered. "And I felt myself die a little every time." His face was bleak, remembering that time. "But I knew he wasn't like his father; not really."

"So you waited." Skade knew Alban had hurt the vampire, but she had never expected *this.*

"I waited," he agreed. "I begged Terrin to break the spell, but he wouldn't. I think... I think he realized he didn't need me anymore."

"What, exactly, did you do for him?" Skade asked, struggling to keep her voice low and warm. She'd thought it would be weeks before she could get him to open up to her, but he had surprised her.

The vampire avoided her gaze. "I used to Dream for him," he whispered. "Before he stole my name. Before Zaira."

"He stole your name?" Skade hadn't thought to ask his name since the Ghost himself had not known it. "How?"

The vampire closed his eyes and shuddered. "I would rather...not go into that, my Lady."

"Call me Skade," Skade said automatically. "Why did he want to replace you with Zaira?" She realized Terrin must have been combing the countryside for years to find one Prophet, much less two. No wonder he had stashed Alban in his brother's Kingdom, and vanished. Had he been planning this since then?

"I lied to him," the vampire whispered, and bowed his head.

"Lied? I've always heard that Prophets..."

"Dream true; I know." He managed a smile, but it didn't last long. "I did Dream true, but I lied to him when he asked. He made Zaira so she wouldn't be *able* to lie, although I imagine Zaira has figured out that she doesn't have to tell the whole truth by now."

Skade smiled. "An ingenious way to get around that problem," she commented dryly. "What did you lie about?"

The vampire hesitated, staring at her as if trying to gauge what her reaction would be.

"You needn't worry," Skade said, trying to placate him. "No judge in the Seven Kingdoms would convict you on any grounds."

"I'm not worried about judges," the vampire said.

"I know." Skade smiled at him.

"Ten years ago, the Royal Family of Abderus was murdered on their way to Cynara's coronation," the vampire whispered.

"I remember that," Skade said, trying to recall where they had been killed. "I was in Severin when I heard the news..." She stared at the vampire with dawning horror. "No."

"He had to do a test, he said," the vampire said helplessly. She could see him flinch away from the memories. "Why do you think Valdis lived this long?"

"Oh, gods, no," Skade whispered. She had never felt so sickened in her entire life, even when she'd seen what Terrin had done to Zaira. Her lips felt stiff and unyielding, as if her body did not want her to voice the tragedy. "He killed them all?"

"He had help, but his helpers died soon after," the vampire whispered.

His face had frozen; Skade could only see the torment in his eyes. She wondered if he had ever told anyone else before.

"No one else knows," the vampire whispered. "Just me." He closed his eyes.

"You're not finished, are you?" Skade asked. "What else happened? What did you lie about?"

"The young Prince was playing in the water as the family and their guards waited for the ferry," the vampire whispered. "When the guards turned on them and struck, he was stabbed and knocked into the river."

His face was so pale that Skade fancied she could see the veins running through his flesh.

"He... Terrin asked me if the Prince had died."

"And what did you tell him?" Skade asked, still horrified, but wanting to know what happened.

The vampire opened his eyes. "I told him yes."

"And that was a lie?" Skade wanted to make sure she understood what he had done.

"He floated downstream, and was found by a fisherman and his wife whose only son had died the winter before," the vampire whispered. "They cared for him until he was well, but evidently he never spoke, and seemed to be damaged somewhere in his mind."

Skade winced.

"When Terrin found out he was still alive--and I didn't tell him--he had the fisherman and his wife killed, and the Prince brought to the place he was staying. The boy wasn't right in the head; he had a vacant look that is too hard to fake, but I had lied to Terrin."

He turned away from her, one hand pressed over his mouth, as if struggling to keep the words from pouring forth. But once the dam had broken, it was very difficult, if not impossible, to stop the flow.

"He made me kill the Prince," the vampire whispered, "and then he stole my name and my powers, and left me a shell of the person I once was."

"But let you remember what you did." Skade couldn't decide which was more horrible, the stolen name and subsequent powers, or the murders themselves.

The vampire turned away from her, and she saw his shoulders hunch. "I'll understand if you don't want me to stay here," he finally whispered. "Sheltering a Prince is one thing, but a murderer..."

Skade wasn't quite sure what she could say to him that he wouldn't take the wrong way. She saw his shoulders tighten even further when she did not immediately reply.

"Why would you think I would abandon you now?" she finally asked. "I didn't allow you the use of my bed and my bathroom to run you out of Iomar when you told me what I wanted to know."

He glanced at her from the corner of his eye, trying to mask the surprise on his face.

"Please turn around." Skade couldn't stand it when people were afraid of her who had no reason to be afraid of her. "I like to see the people I'm talking to."

The vampire hesitated, his fingers twitching for the safety of his cloak again. Skade didn't really want to tell him that her servants had destroyed the cloak; she thought she could come up with another one if he really felt better wearing it.

He slowly turned, his gaze somewhere near her slippered feet.

"Tell me why you think I should drive you out," she suggested. "Then believe me when I answer your reasons with ones of my own."

He remained silent.

"Then let me list my reasons," Skade said, unperturbed. "Did I not ask you what happened? Did I promise you safety here?"

Tears slowly tracked down the sides of his face. Skade remembered what he had been through, and cursed Terrin under her breath. To put a child through this was bad enough, but a *prophet*... Before she could rethink her actions, she crossed the short distance between them and enveloped him in her arms.

He stood there, frozen for a moment, then collapsed against her, sobbing, trying to muffle the sobs in his shirt. His head barely reached her collar bone. Skade's heart filled with a black hate for Terrin and what he had done, not only to the vampire child she held in her arms, but to Alban, his own son; to Teluride, who should have had years to wait until he reigned in Leysan; and to Zaira, who should have had a normal childhood instead of the Hell she had to endure.

She made a silent vow to not stop until Terrin was brought to justice. Whether it be death or the Council of Kingdom's own courts. If she believed what Zaira had said, Terrin would die before he reached a single court.

And Skade would be there to see his destruction.

Chapter 15

Zaira awoke to find the forest around her had been covered with a sparkling sheet of snow; every flake shining like diamonds in the early morning light. She lay under it for a moment, even though the reflection from the snow hurt her eyes, then slowly got to her feet.

Her clothes were soaked through from lying on the cold ground for so long, but the cuts on her hands and feet had finally stopped bleeding, and the swelling seemed to have gone down around her eyes.

She found her father's dagger lying in a pool of melted snow a foot away from the tree that had sheltered her, and she managed to slide it through the ripped waistband of her skirt so it wouldn't get lost. Her stomach growled, but Zaira was used to hunger, so she ignored it and concentrated on the terrain around her.

It had been many years since she'd set foot in any forest. She couldn't quite remember if she ever had. But just the sight of freedom, just the thought that she was finally free, made little things like hunger and the pain in her feet seem all the more unimportant. She knew they *were* important, but she couldn't bring himself to care right now.

She was free.

Briefly, she wondered what her Dreams would say about that. She realized that she had no idea what would happen to her after her escape, and this absence of knowledge both thrilled and frightened her. She decided to try to wait for sleep at night, so she would live in ignorance for a little while longer.

She *liked* not knowing what would happen next.

Zaira slid down a snowy hill to a half-frozen stream, and drank of the pure, cold water, washing the last remnants of blood from her mouth.

She caught a glimpse of her reflection in the shards of ice, and stared.

She knew what Terrin had done to her, and she had seen her reflection in others' eyes, but she had never truly seen her reflection before. Her hands slid over the purple bruises on her face and the matted tangle of her hair. Inexplicably, she felt tears gather in her eyes, and she blinked them away before they could fall.

She touched her hair again, and wondered if it would be best just to cut it all off. She doubted she'd be able to comb it with a dagger, and she had no idea how to carve anything, much less a comb. Her hands moved to her clothes next, spotted with dried blood and other nasty things. Zaira supposed she would look very undesirable should she be seen, and she realized how easy it would be for Terrin to track her.

She imagined Terrin riding into some dirty village, and asking about a beggar child with white hair. Who wouldn't notice her?

First, she would have to do something about the hair. Then she would need to find better clothes, although finding clothes in a forest would prove to be difficult. She had no idea where the nearest village lay.

She'd have to put food in there somewhere, too. She wouldn't be able to go on for long without something to eat.

Zaira washed her hands and feet, careful of the cuts, gasping a little from the cold water. When they were clean, she wrapped her feet in the rags again, and started in on her hair, tearing out tangles that wouldn't be budged when she attempted to comb it with her fingers. Using her reflection as a guide, she managed a wavering cut, and removed the worst of the matted parts, leaving a dirty white behind.

She looked no less strange, but she felt cleaner.

The sun had moved past her tree before she was finished, so she secured the dagger again and followed it. The hunger had faded to a dull roaring in her ears by nightfall.

Zaira found some wrinkled berries still hanging from a dead bush, but she had no idea if they were edible or not, so she left them on the branch and decided to camp under a low-hanging pine.

Late that night she awoke to a crashing in the bushes somewhere near. Nothing disturbed the heavy branches of the pine, so she drifted back to sleep.

Surprisingly, she did not Dream of her escape or what would happen to her next. Her Dream was about Terrin, and what would happen to her father when Terrin discovered she had escaped.

She awoke with tears on her cheeks, even though she could do nothing (save return to Glinyeu, which she knew she'd never do) to save her father's life.

She emerged from under the pine tree and blinked in the sunlight. Whatever had crashed through the brush in the middle of the night had not left any traces behind, save a small mound of something on a flat rock a few feet away. Zaira approached it warily, eyes and ears alert for any sign of a trap. She saw and sensed nothing, but the small pile on the flat rock was a loaf of bread and a bright, shiny red apple.

Zaira's stomach growled, but she didn't touch the food. She sat for a moment and stared at it, trying to think of who would have left it, but her mind, normally so reliable at knowing things, refused to tell her.

She did not know how to check food for poison, so she ate it quickly, still watching the forest. Nothing moved through the trees to capture her; even the birds had vanished and an unearthly stillness lay over everything. Zaira did not like the quiet, so she shoved half of the loaf over the hilt of the dagger and hurried west again, her back prickling as if someone watched her from the silent trees.

The next night, she waited for the crashing sound again, tense and unhappy under another pine tree, but she heard only the normal sounds of a nighttime forest. An owl hooted from the top of a tree a few feet away, and mice scurried through the damp leaves.

She fell into a fitful sleep and dreamed of death again, darker and bloodier dreams than she was used to dreaming.

And when she awoke, someone had laid an outfit outside her tree, evidently moving so silently she hadn't heard them. She picked up a dark green shirt, brown pants, socks, boots, underthings, and a pair of scuffed boots. There was a small wooden comb stuck inside one of the boots, and a bar of sweet-smelling soap in the toe of the other. And there was a brown tweed cloak, just her size.

Now Zaira knew her mysterious benefactor wasn't Terrin or her father. Neither man would have cared if she wore rags; neither would have bothered to feed her before they seized her again. *Who had decided to help her, and what were their motives?* When she discovered that everything fit perfectly, she stood for a moment in the weak sunlight, and tried to stop grateful tears from blurring her vision. She carried the pile down to the creek, stripped only after making certain no one watched her from the trees, and stepped into the freezing water.

Twenty minutes later, panting and blue-lipped, she wore her new clothes, and felt almost warm. She worked on her hair for an hour, silently bearing the pain of combing, but tugging and pulling the tangles out still brought tears to her eyes. She tied her hair back with a cord she found in the pocket of her new pants, slid the dagger through the braided belt, and warmed her hands in the soft wool of the cloak.

She ate the rest of the bread before she started out again, and found a sturdy stick to help her walk instead of slide down the hills to the creek.

Zaira felt the eyes as she walked away from the tree, but this time she didn't bother to look back.

This continued for a week, with Zaira waking up to bread and fruit every morning, and the watcher keeping silent and completely hidden in the trees. She grew to depend on the watcher's gifts, and with regular feeding, she realized she felt much better, too. Her eyesight was sharper, and her eyes were less inclined to water in the brighter sunlight. Her legs strengthened. Her arms, though still stick-thin, developed a wiriness that was more from her daily struggle with the ice on the stream than any exercise.

Zaira felt almost at peace, content for the watcher to stay hidden, content to be alone in the forest with no one to talk to but herself. The Dreams returned after the third day of food, but they refused to show her who the watcher was, or what he or she wanted.

Zaira thought she could live quite nicely by herself in the forest without seeing another human soul, and was totally prepared to do that until she heard the Hounds.

The Hounds. *Terrin's* Hounds, to be exact, which meant Terrin knew she had escaped, and her father was dead. Zaira had heard their howls so many times before that she had occasionally heard them in her sleep.

But she wasn't dreaming now.

She started up from her sheltering tree, eyes wide in the dim moonlight, expecting a Hound to rush from the dark underbrush and take her, but the howls were a mile or two away yet. A mile or two away, but closing fast.

Zaira spun away from the tree, grabbed both stick and dagger, and ran in blind panic away from her shelter. She tripped over three hidden logs and a tree root before she realized she wouldn't get very far in the dark by running away from them in a blind panic.

They howled again, closer now, and Zaira abandoned cold sanity for gibbering hysteria. She turned, blindly, intending to cross the creek and hopefully buy herself a few moments, and almost crashed into a dark figure standing three feet away.

Her breath froze in her throat. Her heart thundered loudly in her ears. She tensed to run, and the figure bent down and seized her shoulders.

"Zaira, don't be afraid." She spoke in a whisper, almost too fast for her to follow. "I'm sorry we had to meet like this, but I'm the one who has been following you and leaving you food. I'd intended to let you make your own way to my cottage, but I fear the Hounds will get you long before then."

Zaira's breath whooshed out in a thin scream. The woman crouched down in front of her, and she desperately tried to pull away.

"Zaira, listen to me. My name is Espen. I was called here by Skade to help Prince Teluride, but I sensed you here in the woods, and decided to help you first."

Zaira knew she was breathing far too fast; the dark woods around her were slowly being replaced by bursts of bright light. She tried to push her panic under control, but she couldn't force the image of the Lady being ravaged by the Hounds from her mind.

"Zaira. I want to *help* you." The woman released her shoulders; she stood in front of her, quivering. "But I can't help you if you don't want me to. It doesn't work that way."

"I didn't Dream of you," Zaira whispered finally, and swayed.

The lady caught her shoulders again, but lightly this time, giving her the option to pull away.

Then she laughed. She had a warm, buttery laugh that tingled down the base of Zaira's spine. "No one can Dream of me, Zaira," she said. "Will you let me help you?"

The panic drained away in a wash of fear, replaced by numbing exhaustion that colored the forest around her with shades of purples and blacks. Zaira closed her eyes, swayed again, and would have fallen if the woman--Espen--hadn't been holding her up.

She heard the Hounds again, but she could not find the strength to flee.

"Yes," she whispered. "Please."

"Then take my hand, and we'll go to my cottage," Espen said, and Zaira gripped her hand, realizing with a start how pale her own hand looked in relation to Espen's. She almost snatched it back.

Espen stopped at the edge of the creek, turned and scented the air like a hound herself. Then she tightened her grip on Zaira's hand, and stepped into the water.

The stream vanished beneath Zaira's feet. She stumbled, almost fell, and felt her hand slip from Espen's grasp. Then the darkness covered her, smothering out sight and sound and feeling, and she let herself fall into the blackness, far too deep for dreams.

"When do you plan to return to Severin?" Skade thought Kyne and Eadda did not look a bit like sisters, although she could see a sort of resemblance in the set of their mouths and their identical noses. They had been together ever since Kyne left Alban in the healers' care, catching up on gossip, she supposed. She hoped Eadda hadn't let anything slip about Zaira.

She hoped the Mirror would be able to find her before Terrin did.

"I'd like to stay until you're certain everyone will live," Kyne said quietly. "How are they?"

Skade wondered who she was more worried about: the vampire, Alban, or Teluride.

"Everyone is still alive," Skade said, seeing no reason not to tell the truth. "And you are free to visit them--except Teluride." Teluride was the worst, of course. Skade hoped Espen would get to Iomar soon so she could look at him. She did not like the fact that he still remembered nothing.

"I would not mind staying here with Kyne," Eadda said softly. "Cynara has our reports, and will understand if we do not return immediately."

Kyne nodded. "And the vampire?"

"He's still in my room," Skade said. "Alive, and whole, or as whole as he can be after what Terrin did to him." *And Alban*, she thought.

"And Alban?" Kyne asked, almost hesitating to speak his name.

"Alive, and full of remorse," Skade said softly. "He doesn't want to forgive himself for what he did to you and the vampire."

She still didn't know what Alban had done to Kyne, and she probably never would. *Alban* probably didn't know; she had felt his urge to block those memories as an almost physical thing.

"Perhaps I should go talk to him," Kyne suggested, not looking at Skade. Eadda stared at her, then at Skade, confused, but didn't comment.

"Perhaps you should," Skade agreed. "You both are welcome here for as long as you want to stay, and I will open a secure portal to Severin as soon as you're ready to leave."

"Thank you, Skade," Eadda said.

"I'll go talk to Alban." Kyne smiled at her sister. "I'll be right back."

Eadda watched her go with a worried frown on her face, but she made no move to stop either Skade or Kyne as they left the room.

As soon as they were outside, Kyne crossed her arms and stared at Skade.

"I know what you want to know, and I'm not going to tell you," she said. "He doesn't even remember."

"Knowing might help me work through his anger at himself once we start to train him," Skade said, her voice equally soft. "But you don't have to tell me anything. He may still remember, eventually."

Kyne's eyes turned to hard shards of ice. Skade felt that she was looking at a stranger; an enemy loose in her own castle. She felt the wards shudder, and stilled them with a thought.

"Pray that he doesn't," Kyne whispered, and her eyes returned to normal. "He will not wish to remember. *I* do not wish him to remember." She paused. "But I will visit him. He did not deserve what his father did to him."

"I'd have to agree with that," Skade said. "This is his room." She opened the door, peeked inside, and found Alban sitting on the edge of his bed, facing the window. He turned around when the door opened, but didn't speak.

"Kyne's here to see you," Skade said. "Can she come in?"

Something--guilt, perhaps?--flickered across Alban's face, but it was gone as quickly as it appeared. He nodded, once, and Skade stepped away from the door.

"Don't hurt him," she warned.

Kyne laughed humorlessly. "I won't harm a hair on his head," she said. "You should know that by now."

"I'm not worried about the hairs on his head," Skade retorted, "I'm worried about his mind."

She left Kyne outside the door, and walked towards her room to check in with the Mirror, trying not to feel like everything was slowly slipping out of her control.

Espen had to contact her soon. If she didn't, Skade would be forced to search her out, and that would be a bit more difficult than finding one small prophet in a forest the size of Abderus.

Terrin had managed to keep Teluride's disappearance from everyone who mattered, the Council especially. No one but himself would miss Alban, and the vampire rarely showed himself in polite company. So he had time, fortunately, to plot the best way to get them from Skade.

What he didn't have, unfortunately, was proof that Skade had them at all.

To call the Queen of Iomar reclusive was almost too trite. Skade usually kept out of mainland affairs--and Terrin couldn't imagine why she would be interested in the injured Prince of Leysan and his traitorous son--and she rarely set foot outside her palace, if the rumors were true. Knowing so little about Skade frustrated Terrin to no end, but he had no one to give him answers, save Zaira, and Zaira was hopefully locked safely away in Glinyeu.

Hopefully. Terrin knew it was only a matter of time before Skade discovered where he had hidden Zaira, and Eabon wasn't the type to lie under pressure. If Skade visited Glinyeu in search of his Dreamer, she would find her. He had no doubt of that.

But he couldn't drop everything and ride to Glinyeu. The Council had to be appeased and kept in the dark, and Terrin had his own crowning to plan.

He wondered if he should invite all the other Kings and Queens, and if Skade would appear if he invited her.

Where had his careful plans gone wrong? How had Alban been able to break free of the spell after it had held him immobile for over a month? How had they broken through the spells he'd woven to hold Teluride captive?

How had his son managed to find such a powerful ally as Skade? Alban had been literally in Terrin's power since the day he had arrived in Leysan with the vampire. His son had never had a chance to contact Skade, and Terrin knew he had not slipped the spell.

Skade must have been working on her own, then. How had she found out about his bid for his brother's throne? And why had she bothered to take the vampire?

The vampire... Terrin frowned. Surely he could use a creature he owned-- body, mind and soul--to get Skade back. Surely he could use the vampire to thwart Skade's plans, whatever they may be. But he could not find his spells or the vampire's consciousness, no matter how hard he tried. Had the destruction of Alban's spell also destroyed Terrin's older ones? How would he be able to regain his prisoners?

What about Alban? Would he be able to rebuild the spell without alerting Skade to his plans? He reached out for the remnants, and felt them fluttering far away, deep inside his son's wounded mind. Terrin smiled and concentrated. The pieces slowly formed back into place, and with careful nudging he thought he might be able to control his son from afar. Blood called to blood, after all. If the vampire had escaped his net, Terrin would have to see to it that Alban did not.

If that didn't drive him mad, or flush his prey from Skade's stronghold, nothing would.

At last he had a plan.

Chapter 16

"You can open your eyes now, Zaira," the witch said, and Zaira heard a current of amusement running through her kind voice. She opened her eyes.

Instead of the dark forest with the Hounds baying at her back, she stood inside a stone cottage filled to bursting with odd sorts of things. There were books on every wall that vied for space with paintings and bottles and baskets and blankets...Zaira couldn't stop staring at it all.

"Welcome to my home," Espen said. "You'll be safe here."

In her borrowed finery, Zaira suddenly felt like an intruder. She dropped her gaze to her feet, and tried to shrink into her cloak. The cottage exuded warmth, but she felt a chill course up her back, making her knees go weak and her eyes burn from unwanted tears. She sank down on the floor.

"Zaira?"

Zaira covered her face with her pale hands, not wanting to look at Espen.

"Zaira, honey, what's wrong?"

Zaira glanced up at her through the shelter of her fingers. The witch had the darkest skin Zaira had ever seen on a person, almost as dark as the chocolate a Lady had once brought her in exchange for information. Her eyes were just as dark, and kind; her hair had been braided into tiny little braids with beads on the end that clinked when she moved.

Zaira thought that she was the most beautiful person she had ever seen, save for, perhaps, Skade. And seeing her only made her more aware of what *she* looked like.

"I've never been safe before," she finally whispered, clutching the cloak around her. What would Espen do when she found out she'd rescued a monster?

"What's wrong, Zaira?" Espen knelt in front of her, ignoring all her fine belongings to focus her attention on Zaira alone. "Tell me. No one will harm you here."

"Do you know who I am?" Zaira asked wretchedly.

"I know who you are." Espen didn't volunteer how she knew this, but Zaira wasn't worried about that. "I know who your father is. I know how you escaped from Glinyeu, and I know how brave you were."

"I'm not brave," Zaira whispered, her head still bowed.

"Hmm." The witch shook her head. "I think I might have to disagree with you about that, Zaira. A lot of people I know wouldn't have survived what you have survived."

Zaira felt a hot tear slip off the end of her nose and plop on the spotless floor. "A lot of people you know don't know the future," she whispered, almost challenging.

"There's that," Espen allowed, and dismissed it. "Why don't you come to the kitchen with me? We can have some lunch and talk."

Zaira stared at her, too shocked to remember she hadn't seen her fully yet. She'd never had someone dismiss her Dreams before. Espen didn't seem to care if she knew the future or not.

Instead of feeling comforted by this, Zaira only felt confused.

"Are you hungry?" Espen asked, her voice still calm.

"Y-yes," Zaira whispered, wondering if she had heard her correctly. She was so used to being taken advantage of, that actually meeting someone who didn't wish her to Dream left her stunned.

Espen reached out one dark hand, and Zaira hesitantly put her pale hand in hers. "Would you like to leave your cloak here?" she asked, "or do you feel more comfortable with it on?"

Zaira hesitated. She felt safe within the folds of the cloak, but it was also slightly warm inside Espen's cottage. She unclasped it, and let it slip from her shoulders, standing there in the sunlight exposed. She felt naked without the cloak.

Espen made no comment on her appearance. "I can show you the bathroom if you want to clean up before we eat," she suggested.

Struck dumb by her indifference, Zaira could only nod. She let Espen lead her into a small but well-appointed bathroom. The witch showed her where the towels were kept, how to pump the water, and left her alone.

Zaira avoided the mirror. She didn't want to see herself clearly, not until she was clean.

The water did not come out of the pump cold, but piping hot, and Zaira wondered if Espen had somehow spelled it to be that way. From the little she remembered of her life before, she thought her nurse had to heat water for a bath over a fire, not pump it into a tub already hot. It took an hour just to wash all the grime from her body, using sweet-smelling soap that stung her eyes.

"I have some clean clothes for you," Espen said from outside the door. "And I'd be happy to cut your hair when you're dressed."

Zaira took the hint, and scrubbed the rest of the dirt away. She dried off, then quickly dressed in the clothes she found piled outside the door. Again, they fit perfectly.

Espen trimmed her hair with a pair of silver scissors, evening out her awkward attempt without one word of dismay. By the time she had finished, Zaira's hair lay straight and fine against the back of her neck, parted in the middle and an inch or two longer than her ears.

"There. How does that look? I had to cut it a bit short to even it out, but..." Espen turned her towards the mirror before she could look away, and she stared, transfixed, at her reflection.

Her skin was white and colorless; her hair the dull ivory of bones. Bruises spotted her face, still painful but not at all puffy. The cuts had healed to thin lines of scabbed-over red, making it look like she had run naked through a briar patch.

Her eyes were a faded green, almost too pale to have color at all. Whatever Terrin had done to her had bleached the color from her body, and left her a pale shadow in return.

Zaira glanced away from the mirror and bowed her head. She felt tears gather in her eyes, but she struggled not to let them fall.

Espen's warmth behind her was the only thing that held her upright. She placed one dark hand on Zaira's shoulder and gave her a little squeeze.

"The bruises should fade in the next few days," she said. "I made pancakes, and I have fresh bread, apple butter, and scrambled eggs to go with them."

Zaira's stomach growled. She cast another glance at the specter in the mirror, and saw a faint flush rise to her cheeks. "Thank you," she whispered.

Espen laughed. "You're welcome. Shall we go?"

Feeling oddly light, as if the removal of dirt and the tangles of her hair had released something deep inside her soul, Zaira followed her to the sunny kitchen and sat in the proffered chair. A black and white cat appeared from somewhere and rubbed against her legs. Zaira wasn't quite sure what to do. The cat meowed.

"Her name is Jess," Espen said. "She likes to be petted."

Jess' fur was soft and thick as Zaira ran her fingers over her back. When she straightened up, a plate full of food had appeared in front of her, and she forgot about the cat long enough to pick up a fork and work at quenching her hunger.

Espen did not question her through the meal, but settled back with a plate of her own and a cup full of tea from the pot on the stove. It was a strange looking stove, white and gleaming like nothing Zaira had ever seen. And she brought her milk out from an icebox that was as strange as the stove, white and tall and with no ice in evidence.

The rest of the cottage, at least the parts Zaira had seen, looked normal, save for the amount of books. She had never seen so many books in her life.

"Why did you rescue me?" she finally asked, full of drowsy contentment now that her hunger was sated. She pushed her plate away and leaned back in her chair.

"That's what I do," Espen replied. "I rescue people. I would have been here earlier, but we're a bit short-handed right now, and I was in the middle of a mess somewhere else."

"Somewhere else?" Zaira asked curiously. She had Dreamed of no other trouble in the whole of Cruinne, and she would have remembered anything not fitting in with Terrin's plans.

Espen stared at her for a moment, as if trying to gauge how much she should tell her. "A friend of mine was in trouble," she finally said. "I had to go a long way to help him. When I got Skade's message, I came here as quickly as I could." She paused and sipped her tea. "But then I saw you, and you obviously needed help."

"The Hounds would have found me," Zaira whispered. Although she hadn't Dreamed of this, she knew it was true. The Hounds would have found her and killed her, or dragged her back to Glinyeu and the horrible little room.

"Yes, they would have," Espen agreed. "Skade called me here because of Teluride. Do you know anything about him?"

Zaira shrugged. "Terrin blamed King Valdis's death on Teluride," she said. "The spell he used on Teluride made him lose his memory, so no one knows if he's guilty or not." *No one except for me and Terrin,* she thought silently, but didn't offer that thought to Espen.

"I'm not sure if I remember Terrin," Espen said, frowning. "It's been a while since I've been here."

"Where else is there to go?" Zaira asked. She had never Dreamed of other lands, but she supposed they must exist if Espen had been to them.

Espen smiled. "Oh, there are many places to go," she said. "More than you can dream about or imagine. Would you mind filling me in? If you'd rather not tell me, I can always contact Skade, and hear everything from her."

Zaira had already begun to speak before she was finished. She only got as far as the murder before Espen held up her hand to silence her.

"Do you have to answer every question someone asks of you?" she said after studying her for a long moment.

"Yes." Zaira saw no reason to lie. Espen could find out from Terrin or anyone who had come to question her.

"Then I will have to be careful what I request," Espen said softly. "I'm sorry if I took advantage of your talent, Zaira. I'll try my best not to do it again."

Zaira stared at her, openmouthed. No one--*no one*--had ever apologized to her before. "You don't..." she began, but Espen shook her head.

"Yes, I do," she said. "I should have asked you what the consequences were before I asked you any questions."

Although Zaira felt very at ease around the witch, she could not seem to fathom why she seemed so worried about her feelings. No one else had ever asked her permission or opinion about anything, save for her Dreams. Why should she care? She took a sip of tea to cover her confusion and shrugged.

"No one else ever did."

"I know." Her expression softened. "If I had known about you earlier..." She seemed genuinely upset, but Zaira couldn't understand why. She had not Dreamed of her; Espen's appearance was a complete surprise.

She said as much, not meeting her eyes, and took a slice of bread so she would have something to do with her hands.

"I know," Espen said. "But still, I could have..." she shook her head, "I should contact Skade, and tell her I'm here. Do you mind?"

"Don't you want to know what happened?" Zaira asked. "I don't mind telling you." She realized in surprise that she really *didn't* mind telling her anything. Espen seemed so calm and dependable, like the mother she did not remember. Zaira would have been happy to stay in her cottage for the rest of her life.

Espen shook her head. "I'm not going to use you like that, even if you don't mind," she said. "Skade can tell me; it will give her a chance to let me know how good a job she's done." She grinned. "Skade's not a bad person, for a Queen, but she does like to brag."

Zaira mirrored her smile. "I know."

Espen cleared the table, and set the dishes in the sink to soak. "I think that's the first time I've seen you smile," she said. "You should do it more often. It suits you."

Embarrassed, Zaira glanced down at the table and ran one pale finger through a puddle of water from her glass.

Espen did not press the point. When she looked up, she saw that she had placed a mirror on the table between them. She could only see the back of it, not the surface, but she could feel a faint sense of magic around it, akin to the feeling she received from Terrin's spells.

"You can come around to the front if you would like to say hello," Espen said. Zaira slid from her chair and moved around to the front of the mirror. She peered over Espen's shoulder, ready to duck down if anyone other than Skade appeared.

The mirror showed no reflections. Instead, its surface rippled slightly, as if it were underwater. And as Zaira watched, the rippling grew more pronounced and a glow emanated from the center of the mirror, expanding outward until she could see a room and a figure lying on a narrow bed. Zaira recognized him at once, but Espen frowned and shook her head.

"It's the vampire," Zaira offered.

"I see. But where is Skade?" She didn't mean to ask her that question; she knew that, but it didn't matter. Once asked, Zaira would know, Dream or no Dream.

"She'll..." *be coming through the door in a minute*, she would have said, but Espen turned her head and stared at her until she stuttered into silence.

A wavering figure appeared in the mirror, blocking their view of the room. "She's not here," the Ghost whispered. "Do you want me to take a message?" He stared out of the mirror at Espen. Zaira saw his gray face freeze, then he frowned as if trying to remember where he had seen her before.

Espen stared at the gray figure in the mirror, shock mingled with pity on her face. Zaira risked a glance at the Ghost, but couldn't see anything to pity him for. No one had ever asked her about the Ghost in the mirror, so she had no idea who he was, or why Espen would be so shocked.

"Skade, do you realize what you've done?" She shook her head, collected herself with a visible effort, and managed to smile at the gray-faced figure. "We'll wait."

The Ghost nodded and faded away, but not before giving Espen another puzzled glance. As if he recognized her, but didn't quite know who she was, Zaira thought. As if he had lost his memory, and was only now finding it again.

She didn't have a chance to ask Espen about the Ghost, and she did not ask him. Skade walked through the door a moment later, and Zaira was instantly transfixed by the face that had haunted her Dreams for so long: the lovely Queen of Iomar, herself.

Alban sat on the broad windowsill and stared out at the Kingdom of Iomar. He could not see the streets below; the rain fogging the window and his own breath saw to that, but he could imagine the fabled city as a wonderful thing. He pulled his knees up to his chest and buried his head in his arms. He did not feel as if he belonged in this peaceful place.

A quiet knock on the door forced him to raise his head, but he hesitated before calling out that the door was open. Kyne appeared in the doorway, composed and dressed in borrowed finery: a short dark green jerkin and a pair of black pants. Her boots rose to her knees, black as well, and supple. Although she wore no visible weapons, Alban doubted she had agreed to walk through Iomar unarmed.

"How do you feel?" she asked, her voice soft in the silence. "Skade asked me to come."

Alban's face felt stiff when he opened his mouth to answer her. "I feel much stronger," he said honestly. "How is your sister?" He vaguely remembered Skade or one of the nurses telling him about Eadda, but he couldn't recall if they had mentioned anything else.

Kyne smiled. "She will recover," she said, and hovered in the doorway, at a loss for words.

Alban slid down from his perch and hesitated. "I'm sorry for what I did to you," he whispered. "I don't know what I did, but I can't help but feel..."

"It was nothing lasting," Kyne said. "I'm just glad we got out of Leysan before your father returned. Has Skade asked what you want to do?"

"Stay as far away from Leysan as possible," Alban said, with a shudder. If he could live out the rest of his life without ever seeing his father again, he'd be happy.

"Hopefully that will be possible," Kyne said. She moved further into the room and sat on the edge of his bed. Alban stayed near the window. "If things go well, and Eadda and I return to Severin, I would not be adverse to you accompanying us."

"To Severin?" Alban blinked. He had not expected this at all.

Kyne smiled. "You could get quite an education in Severin," she said. "My sister has an extensive body of wizards on her staff. I'm sure they would be happy to train you."

"I'll have to think about it," Alban whispered. He thought he should add more, but he couldn't think of anything else to say.

"Of course," Kyne said. "I'll ask you again before we leave. Until then, rest and regain your strength."

Before Alban could reply, she was gone, closing the door behind her, and leaving him in darkness again.

He eventually settled back on the windowsill, but the rainy streets of Iomar outside held no magic for him now. His heart was too troubled for thoughts of Skade's beautiful city.

"Skade!" the Ghost appeared as soon as she stepped through the doorway, and at first she thought he had found Zaira dead somewhere in the forest. She glanced at the vampire, who lay on her bed asleep, but saw nothing wrong with him.

"There's no need to shout," she finally said. "What's wrong? Did you find Zaira?"

"Indirectly," the Ghost replied. "Espen is here to speak with you, but may I ask you a question before you talk to her?"

A question? Skade stared at him for a moment. He almost looked...frightened, she finally decided. But his fear wasn't because of her, for a change, but from something else.

"Yes, you may," she allowed. "One question."

"I...I recognized Espen," the Ghost whispered. "And she recognized me. But I do not know her. Should I?"

Whatever possible questions she had expected, Skade had not expected *this*. She opened her mouth to answer him, then realized she honestly didn't know what to say. "You knew Espen in your previous...life," she said. "But you shouldn't have recognized her at all."

"I would rather not, my Lady," the Ghost whispered. "I think...whatever I did to become your prisoner..." he bowed his head, "I think I would rather not know her at all."

Before Skade could reply to that, he faded from view, and Espen's familiar face appeared in the mirror. She dismissed the Ghost's problems for the moment, and concentrated on the task at hand.

"Espen! I've been trying to reach you for..." Skade stopped as soon as she saw the slight, pale figure of Zaira standing behind Espen. The bruises that dotted the child's pale skin made Skade even more furious at Terrin. "I see you found Zaira."

The child reddened and twisted away, obviously ill at ease.

Espen smiled back at her before she replied. "Yes. I found her wandering in the forest. Terrin's Hounds were after her, so I couldn't leave her there for long."

"I'm glad she's safe," Skade said truthfully. "I wanted to talk to you about Teluride, really. Everyone else seems to be recovering nicely."

"Zaira filled me in a little," Espen said. "He's lost his memory?"

The mirror flickered briefly, skewing Espen's features. When it settled down, Zaira had vanished from behind Espen, but Skade saw her standing over by the kitchen counter, trying not to look like she was paying attention. She almost smiled.

"Yes. As far as my healers can tell, his memory is completely gone," Skade said. "They had to tell him his name, back in Leysan. I'm not sure how Terrin managed to do it, but without Teluride's memory, we'll never know if he is guilty or innocent of his father's murder."

In the background, Zaira opened her mouth to speak, decided against it, and closed it again. Skade's interest piqued. "Unless you know?" She directed her question at Zaira.

Skade knew that Espen had seen through her attempt. "I refuse to let you use Zaira like that, Skade," she snapped, but the damage had already been done. "I didn't rescue her from the forest to treat her the same way Terrin has."

"Nor do I expect you to," Skade said coolly, fixing her gaze on Zaira. "But sometimes, in war, you have to make certain concessions."

"I don't mind," Zaira whispered from behind Espen. "Espen, I really don't mind." She twisted the hem of her borrowed shirt, and made as if to step towards the mirror again. Skade held her breath. If Teluride were guilty, she could probably blame it on Terrin and be done with it, but if he were innocent, and *Terrin* was accused of the crime...

Espen turned around. "I will not have your talents exploited. You've been hurt enough."

Zaira wouldn't meet her eyes. "I don't mind," she said again. "Skade needs to know."

"Very well," Espen sighed. "If you feel up to it, you may answer Skade's questions. And then," she fixed Skade with a bemused glare, "we'll talk about Teluride."

Skade beamed. "Thank you. Zaira, did Teluride kill his father?"

"No."

Skade waited for more, but Zaira only bit her lip and glanced unhappily at the mirror.

"He's sick," Zaira offered, "but he didn't kill his father."

"I knew it!" Skade beamed at Zaira, who gave her a wavering smile in return. The smile lit up her face and made her almost beautiful. "I have your diary, Zaira. Do you want it back?"

Zaira shrugged. "I guess I don't need it anymore. You can keep it if you want to."

Skade glanced back at the vampire. He had not awakened since she had helped him to bed the previous night; unburdening himself had evidently been more exhausting than helpful. Now that she knew Teluride was innocent, she could go on from there, but she felt she should ask Zaira another question. What else did she want to know?

"Will he recover?" she asked.

Zaira struggled with this question for a long minute, her face grave. "I'm not sure," she finally whispered. "I think, perhaps, it is too far into the future for me to tell. Terrin always asked me about things that would happen soon."

"I'll do my best, of course," Espen interrupted. "Skade, can he hear us?"

For a short moment, Skade had no idea who she was talking about. Espen tapped the mirror suggestively. "Oh. Yes, more than likely."

"I'll want to talk to you about him later, then," Espen said. "On another mirror, perhaps."

"He's helped me out quite a bit," Skade said, for the Ghost's benefit if he *was* listening in. Espen fixed her with a look she chose to not interpret.

"Do you want to know anything else?" Zaira asked timidly, staring quizzically at Espen.

"Yes, actually, two more questions," Skade said. "First, I want to know a bit more about your...talent. If you are asked something, you have to answer, correct?"

"If I'm asked a question, I know the answer," Zaira clarified.

"So if no one has asked you a question..."

"And I haven't Dreamed it, I wouldn't know the answer," Zaira said.

"Good." Skade glanced back at the vampire again. "Second question. Do you know the vampire's name? Terrin stole it from him along with his powers and his memories. I'd like to give it back to him, if I can."

Zaira opened her mouth to reply, then hesitated. "If you give him his name, Terrin's power over him will be broken, and his memories will return," she whispered.

"That's what I thought," Skade said. "Good. Will you tell it to me?"

Zaira hesitated again. "If you tell him his name, *years* of Terrin's spells will be broken," she said. "His memories will come rushing back."

"What are you trying to say, Zaira?" Espen asked, turning around to glance at her.

"His mind might not hold up under the strain," Zaira whispered.

Skade glanced back at the sleeping vampire. "Oh. Do you think..."

"You said two more questions, Skade," Espen warned.

"One more, and then I'll talk to you about Teluride," Skade promised. "Zaira, what will happen if I tell the vampire his name?"

Zaira closed her eyes. "He will die," she whispered. Her voice barely carried through the mirror. Before Skade could ask her to elaborate, Zaira vanished from her view, slipping out of Espen's kitchen like a ghost child, her pale hair wafting behind her.

"About Teluride," Espen said, after a moment of silence.

"Terrin gave him some sort of drug," Skade explained, watching the mirror closely just in case Zaira returned. "He's stable now, but he still doesn't remember a thing."

"I will do what I can for him, but I can't give you any promises," she said. "You know how these things work."

"I can anchor a portal through a mirror, if you have one big enough to fit him through," Skade said. "The alternative is to send a group to the mainland to deliver him, but with Terrin around, I don't think that would be wise."

"I'm sure I can find a mirror large enough somewhere in this mess," Espen said. "Zaira can help me look."

"Espen, is she in earshot?"

Espen glanced over her shoulder, then shook her head. "She's not in the hallway, at least. I can't guarantee she won't overhear, though. What do you want?"

"How long are you going to keep her there?" Skade asked.

"However long it takes for Zaira to stop being afraid of herself," Espen replied. "And however long she wants to stay. You know full well I cannot force anyone to stay here."

"She'd be safer here," Skade murmured, glancing at the vampire.

Espen snorted. "So you could pepper her with questions you don't need to know the answers to? I don't think so." She stood; evidently the conversation was over. "Give me a day to find a big enough mirror and prepare a bed for Teluride." Her image in the mirror faded before Skade could reply.

Chapter 17

Alban dreamed.

"Do you want to know what you did to the assassin?" Terrin turned from an unfamiliar window and smiled at his son. "I can tell you everything."

Alban stepped back, a sick rush of fear cutting off any strength he might have had. "I...I don't want to know," he whispered.

Terrin smiled. "But I shall tell you, nonetheless," he said. "Do you want to know what else you did?"

"What else?" Alban asked faintly. He felt rough wood behind him...a door, and tried to find the latch.

"Did you really think I'd kill my own brother?" Terrin stepped away from the window and held out his hand. "Come now, Alban. Surely you can't be that naïve."

Fear clutched at Alban's heart. "What do you mean?" he gasped. "I didn't...I couldn't have..." Even as he said that, he realized he very well could have. He didn't remember what he had done to Kyne, even now.

Terrin smiled again. "Oh, but you did. On my order, you did."

"No..."

"Yes."

Alban awoke with a scream trapped in his throat, and tears on his cheeks. *Had* he killed the King? He pushed himself up and stared into the darkness. He didn't feel like a murderer, but from what he dimly remembered about his father's spell, he wouldn't, would he?

Sickened, Alban climbed out of bed and padded over to the window. A sliver of moon peered out from behind a swath of tattered clouds, making the puddles on the street below sparkle and dance.

It was a beautiful scene, but he did not feel calmed. He did not feel at peace.

Had he killed King Valdis? Had *he*, not Terrin, snuck into the King's chambers and stabbed him to death?

He stared down at his hands, and expected to see blood caked on his fingers, but they were clean and pale.

Alban sighed and traced the path of a raindrop down the pane of glass. Perhaps it *had* only been a dream. He glanced longingly back at his bed, but he felt no tug towards sleep. In fact, he was wide-awake now, distressingly so.

He stared down at his hands again. Making the light reappear took an hour of experimentation, but once he saw the green light begin to play across his fingers, he knew he would not forget how to call the light again. He played with it silently for a while, making it dim and brighten with a whim, then banished it, suddenly tired.

Magic evidently took a lot of strength, and he had not recovered yet.

He wondered if he ever would. Surely Terrin would call up an army to attack Iomar before Alban could learn anything. Surely *something* would happen to prevent him from ever mastering what powers he possessed.

He curled up on the windowsill, closed his eyes and leaned his forehead against the cool glass.

He would only rest for a moment, then he would climb back into bed.

"Do you want to know what else you did?" Terrin asked in his mind.

Alban whimpered and tried to twist away from his father's voice, but it followed him down into the darkest echoes of forgotten nightmares.

A week later, Teluride was gone, safe in Abderus with Espen and Zaira. Skade had seen Kyne and Eadda off, laden with news, supplies, fresh horses, and the admonition to be careful.

She had offered to send them through the mirror, but Cynara evidently didn't have one large enough for a portal.

That left Alban and the vampire in Iomar, and Skade worried about them both.

Alban, in particular, had taken to locking his door at night; something she did not normally protest. But considering the fact that he *had* been under a very powerful spell less than two weeks before, she thought it would be better if he stayed in the open, around other people where his father couldn't find him again. Her protections around Iomar were vast, that much was true, but not indestructible. With his previous influence over his son, Terrin could conceivably find a way inside.

Skade knocked on Alban's door, barely able to maneuver the tray of food one of the kitchen staff had given her. *It was due time they had a little talk*, she thought. *He couldn't avoid her forever.*

Alban opened the door a crack, and stiffened when he saw who stood on the other side.

"I brought us supper, and I thought it was high time we talked." Skade pushed past him before he could protest, and set the tray on the bedside table.

"What do you want to talk about?" Alban asked softly. He seemed very ill at ease, his face paler than she remembered, and his eyes fever-bright. Surreptitiously, she probed his mind for any trace of a spell. The traces were there, but she couldn't get past her own wards to follow them back to their source.

"I came to see how you were feeling," Skade said. "I thought supper would be a good way to talk about your future."

"My future?" Alban echoed.

"What do you plan to do now?" Skade asked. "You have options; many options, really, but I'd like you to consider my suggestions first."

Alban blinked. Skade wondered if he had somehow been drugged, or if the breaking of Terrin's spell had truly taken so much out of him. Or did he truly expect her to send him out unarmed and untrained to be captured by his father again?

She realized she had slightly abandoned him, what with Teluride's continuing amnesia, Eadda and Kyne's departure, and the vampire's continuing expectation that she would turn him over to judge, jury, and executioner.

"Are you feeling okay?" she asked, when he didn't reply to her question.

He blinked again. "I haven't been...sleeping well."

"I can have the kitchen send you up a tea that will help you sleep," Skade offered. She supposed she'd have nightmares, too, if she were in his position. "Would that help?"

Alban shrugged. He looked like he wasn't having any trouble taking care of himself, at least; his clothes were clean and he smelled faintly of herbal soap. Skade had heard two of the laundry maids giggling over his purported good looks three days before, but right now he merely looked exhausted.

"Or how about if I send someone up with the tea now?" she asked. "We can talk later, if that would make you feel any better."

He sat down on the edge of his bed, head down, ignoring the food she had brought. Skade stared at him for a moment, then rang the bell for a maid.

"Alban, I can't do a thing for you if I don't know what you want," Skade said softly. "Will you talk to me?"

He rubbed one hand over his eyes and sighed. "Yes. I'll talk to you." His voice was almost inaudible.

"What do you want to do?" she asked, sitting beside him on the bed.

"I... I haven't really thought about it," Alban whispered. "I feel...*wrong*, somehow. As if I'm waiting for something bad to happen." He hazarded a glance at her when he said this, as if he expected her to laugh at him.

Skade made it a point not to laugh at anyone who didn't truly and honestly deserve it.

"I think you're still in shock," she said. "Getting you here was hard enough, but you have to think about your future, as well. No one died getting you here, Alban, so you have nothing to feel guilty for."

He started at the word 'guilty', and she knew she had chosen correctly.

"King Valdis died," he mumbled, looking away.

"That's true," Skade allowed. "But you didn't kill him."

"How do you know?" Alban asked harshly, his face still turned away. "I could have easily killed him. I don't remember anything else my father made me do under that spell." He shivered as he said this, as if just saying the words made them truth.

Skade sat still for a moment, finally realizing what had been bothering him for so long. "You think *you* killed Valdis?" she finally asked, "How? Do you remember something? Why would you want to kill him? He was like a father to you, Alban."

Alban shrugged. "I did something to Kyne I still don't remember. I took the vampire's last source of life away from him." He stared up at her with pain-filled eyes. "I don't remember any of it. If my father had told me to murder the King, who's to say I didn't do it?"

Skade shook her head. "I can't believe you would do it, spell or no spell," she said, but she also realized what he said was true. He *could* have murdered Valdis, and then buried that memory so deep in his mind that it would be practically irretrievable. But she still couldn't believe...

"There's only one way to find out," she said slowly. "If you ask my mirror, and open your mind to it, we'll all know if you're guilty or not."

"And if I'm guilty?" Alban asked harshly.

"Then you killed Valdis under duress, Alban," Skade said patiently. "No one would condemn you for it." *Unless you condemn yourself, which you seem to be doing,* she finished silently, staring at him.

He didn't reply.

"Think about it," she said gently, rising to answer the knock on the door. She took the proffered mug from the red-haired maid, and thanked her quietly. "Drink this."

He stared into the depths of the cup for a moment, as if attempting to puzzle out his actions in the tea leaves, then brought the cup to his lips.

Skade knew from experience that the tea tasted quite palatable. She smiled at him encouragingly when he gave her a questioning look over the mug.

"Drink up," she suggested. "I'll come back tomorrow after you've had a good night's sleep, and we can talk further then."

When he finally lowered the cup, he looked no less troubled, but his eyes were clear and sane. "Thank you," he whispered awkwardly. "I know I haven't been the best of..."

Skade placed one hand over his and squeezed. "Nonsense. You've had a huge shock. You're tired. I understand. Truly I do." Impulsively, she slipped a beaded bracelet from one arm and held it out to him. "Take this, and wear it always. If you're ever in need of my aid, I will be able to help you through it, more often than not."

Alban took the bracelet, and gave her a half-hearted smile. She waited until he had slipped it on his wrist before letting herself out.

He did not lock the door behind her.

Chapter 18

Over the course of the past week, Terrin had cast his net tighter and tighter over his son. He had managed to piece together most of his spell, unknown to both Alban and Skade. It was exhausting work.

He had visited Alban's dreams every night, and sowed the seeds of uncertainty in his mind. Now all he had to do was wait until Alban walked close enough to one of Skade's mirrors for Terrin to take him. The Queen of Iomar would hesitate to cross him again.

Teluride, unfortunately, seemed to be permanently out of reach. Terrin had no idea who Espen was, and no way to find out where in Abderus her cottage lay. He knew the mysterious witch had Zaira as well, and the loss of his prophet irked him even more than the loss of the Prince. He had been forced to disclose the prince's disappearance to the Council, who were fast becoming more and more suspicious. He would have to do something about them soon.

But first, he needed Alban. Without his son, he would not be able to cloud the Council's minds for long. They were already questioning him, and he did not need their questions now.

Someone knocked on the door. Terrin opened his eyes and frowned; it should have been too late for any of the servants to disturb him.

It wasn't a servant; it was the youngest member of the Council.

"The Council requests your presence at an...emergency meeting, my Lord," the man said stiffly. "We wish to discuss your status, now that the Prince has vanished."

"My status?" Terrin asked softly. What were they planning? Surely they did not intend to hold the crown from him? He tested the spell around Alban. Would he be able to pull power from his son if the Council needed to be punished? He thought, perhaps he could.

"The Council isn't certain your crowning should be held so soon after King Valdis' death and the prince's disappearance," the man said. Terrin wished he could remember his name. "There's already talk in the villages..."

"Peasants talk," Terrin said sharply. "But I will attend your meeting."

The young man smiled. "Good. We were hoping you would not already be asleep."

Terrin followed him down the hallway to the Council's meeting room. They were all assembled, six men in all. Three were bumbling fools; one was too young to know any better. The last two had been the King's most trusted advisors, and were more dangerous than the others.

If things got bad enough, Terrin thought he would have to kill them first.

He made sure to lock the door behind him, just in case. It would not do well to have a servant walk in at the most inopportune moment.

"Thank you for coming at such short notice, Lord Terrin," the eldest Council member quavered, shifting a little on his seat. "Did young Darius tell you why we are here?"

"He did," Terrin said, and took his proper seat at the head of the table. "And I can't say I don't agree with you, save for one small thing."

"And what would that be?" Cedrych was one of the dangerous ones, and Terrin knew he was suspicious. He didn't think the blame would fall on himself, but Cedrych still could not believe the prince had murdered his own father, for whatever reason.

"The longer the kingdom goes without a king, the harder it will be to mend the damages," Terrin said smoothly. "Teluride cannot be king if he murdered my brother." He stressed the word 'brother' slightly, reminding them all of his status. "And if we do not find him, he might not live long enough to become a problem."

One of the Council members drew in a sharp breath. Obviously, that thought had not occurred to many of them.

"He was not well, we all knew that," Darius said softly. Terrin vaguely remembered some sort of friendship between the youngest council member and the prince, but he couldn't worry about friendships now.

He had a feeling he'd have to get rid of the Council soon, if not tonight. He tested the spell again, found his son awake and troubled in his faraway sanctuary, and readied himself for the blow he'd have to strike. Cedrych and Alyn first, he thought. Then Darius, then the others.

"I could use some refreshment," he said, and rose. "Permit me to pour you some wine." He crossed the room to the small credenza set against one wall, opened the liquor cabinet, and removed seven cut crystal glasses. He slipped a small parcel of white powder into the carafe, made sure the poison had dissolved, and carried it all to the council table.

"If we do not find the prince, and his guilt is never proved, the kingship will have a pall over it," Alyn argued, pouring himself a cup. "We *must* find him first. Then we can act."

"We all know every kingdom in Cruinne has enemies," one of the weaker members cautioned. "If the ones who wish to abolish kingship entirely find the prince..."

"Then all will be lost," Terrin said, slipping a hint of a spell between his words. He had no time to bicker with an outdated Council. He had yet to act against Alban tonight, and he hoped to have his son back in Leysan by the end of the week. He did not need the Council to rule the kingdom, and Terrin thought it was time the Council realized that. "If we do not act soon, the enemies you speak of will think both Council and King weak. And weakness cannot be tolerated." He waited until they all had wine, then poured himself a glass.

"Still, I must insist on caution..." Alyn's voice faded. He rubbed at his throat. "I think..." He coughed and tugged at the tight collar of his shirt, undoing one button, but it did not help.

Terrin watched impassively as the others exhibited the same symptoms. Only Darius had not touched his wine, and now he stared at it suspiciously, but still not suspicious enough.

"Alyn? Cedrych? Are you ill?" Darius pushed back his chair and went to the nearest man. Alyn's face was purple now, his eyes bulging out as he struggled to breathe. "Lord Terrin, I..." His voice trailed away as he realized what had happened. Darius drew himself up, ever the lordling. "What did you do?"

Terrin shrugged, ignoring the thrashing of the remaining Council members. The eldest was already dead, slumped over his wine like a drunkard at a common tavern.

"The Council has outlived its usefulness," he said softly. "As have you. Drink your wine, Darius."

Darius backed away from the table, his hands upraised in front of him. *As if that would help him live,* Terrin thought, and rose.

"You won't leave this room alive," he said, his voice still soft. "And I don't have all night to hunt you down. I'll give you a choice. Bow to me, submit yourself to me, or die."

"Did you kill the king, too?" Darius asked. Anger born of helplessness fluttered through his eyes. He moved back towards the door and found it locked.

Terrin held up the key. "Submit to me, or I'll make certain you are blamed for this and hanged."

Darius blanched. "You wouldn't dare."

Terrin regarded him quizzically, one eyebrow cocked. "But why wouldn't I?" he mused aloud. Actually, it *would* be an easy answer to the Teluride's disappearance. "You killed the Council before I arrived, and of course you intended to murder me, as well. What did they offer you, Darius? Money? Gold?"

"No one offered me..." Darius eased away from the door as Terrin approached. "*You* are the traitor; not I."

Terrin smiled. "We are the only two people in Leysan who know that, Darius. My brother is dead. My nephew is missing. Even my son is gone, but not for much longer." He took strong hold of the reigns of his spell, and pulled a strand of power away from his son. Alban did not seem to notice at first.

Darius didn't seem to know what to say to save himself. He stood frozen, mouth working in silent amazement as he realized all of the deceptions and lies that had led up to the King's death.

"Did Teluride kill his father?" he finally asked.

Terrin smiled. "What do you think?"

With a low moan, Darius sank down on the floor, his head in his hands. "We believed every word you spoke. We believed every plot you set in motion."

"Yes. And you believed it all so very well," Terrin said, and fashioned a spell out of borrowed power.

In Iomar, Alban stiffened and started to rise from his perch on the windowsill, but his legs folded under him, and he fell heavily to the floor.

Terrin ignored his son's weakness, and threw the spell at Darius. It caught him full in the face. He reared back, screaming as it ate into his skin, leaving raw flesh behind.

He didn't scream for very long. As soon as he had stopped twitching, Terrin left the Council room and hurried back to his own rooms, determined to have Alban back in Leysan by daybreak.

He had a lot to do, now that the Council was gone.

Chapter 19

"Why don't we take a walk in the garden?" Skade pretended she had just thought of this outing, but she didn't think the vampire was fooled.

He started to demur as he had every other time she had suggested he step outside of her room. This time she was prepared to wear him down until he agreed to accompany her.

"You need to get out of here," she said. "No one will harm you here; you know that."

He sighed and would not meet her eyes. "I know."

"Then what are you afraid of?"

The vampire shrugged.

"Please. Don't make me beg you to come," Skade said. "I'd like to show you my roses." She supposed the garden had roses by now; she had not been able to relax anywhere for weeks.

"Roses." He stared at her, disbelieving. "In the dark."

"There's a nice full moon," Skade pointed out. "And moonlight won't kill you; sunlight will."

He couldn't refute this logic, and it was much easier just to comply. Still, he hesitated.

"I can't imagine you were this argumentative with Terrin," Skade commented dryly.

The vampire flushed. "No. No, I wasn't."

"Do I have to beg you to come?"

He finally met her eyes. He must have liked what he saw there, for he finally sighed, then nodded. "I'll come."

Skade smiled. "Good." She held out her hand, and he took it cautiously. "I think you'll like my garden."

On the walk through the castle, he stayed very close to her, even though they met no one on the journey. It was too late for most of the servants, and the other members of Skade's household had gone to bed long ago.

He relaxed once they stepped outside, but only marginally. If he had been alive, he would have worried himself into an ulcer by now, Skade thought sourly, and touched his arm. He jumped.

"Walk with me."

"What do you want to...?"

"Hush." He quieted, instantly fearful. Skade sighed. "Why are you so frightened still? Have I done *anything* to harm you?"

He looked away. "No."

"Then talk to me," she suggested. "Tell me what you wish to do now that you are free."

"I won't be truly free until Terrin is dead," the vampire whispered.

"True." They walked along the pebbled paths in silence for a moment, and Skade tried to remember where the roses were. "But there are ways for you to protect yourself, you know. You don't have to live in fear until he dies."

"I don't know how else to live," the vampire whispered, and stopped, as if he couldn't believe what he had just said. He stared at her. His expression was hard to read in the moonlight, but Skade could easily guess what it was.

"Well, then, if you decide to stay here, I'll do my best to show you," she promised. "Deal?" She held out her hand.

He hesitated, still staring at her. "Deal," he finally whispered, and shook.

"Now. I have a question for you," Skade said, remembering Zaira's dire words about what would happen if the vampire ever discovered his name. "How badly do you want to know your past?"

The vampire hesitated. "Terrin took my name, and with it, who I am. I have no past."

"But you could have one," Skade said. "I had intended to ask Zaira for your name, but she insisted I get your permission first."

The vampire's eyes glittered in the moonlight. "She did?"

"She said you would die if you knew your name," Skade admitted. "I cannot say whether she is right or wrong, but..."

"I don't want to die." He drew away from her when she said this, and stared blindly at the dark rosebushes that surrounded them.

"I know." Skade purposely kept her voice light. "But if I'm *ever* going to be able to stop Terrin, I might just need your help."

He was silent beside her, neither dismissing nor agreeing with her reasoning. Skade thought she could be happy with that, for now, at least.

Before she could broach the subject of giving him a room of his own so she could sleep in her own bed again, she felt something ripple through the beads around her neck. A wash of magic from somewhere shivered across her chest, causing her heart to beat erratically for a long moment.

The vampire stiffened. "What was that?"

Skade rubbed her throat, and shook the beads around her neck. "I'm not sure, but it didn't feel very friendly. Perhaps we should go in."

"I think it came from your Mirror," the vampire whispered, staring up at the castle. "I thought I recognized the feeling..." He started forward without giving Skade a chance to evaluate the feeling before she rushed into action.

"Wait," she said, and he stopped, his back to her. "What do you know about my Mirror?"

He shrugged. "Only that the Ghost is your prisoner. Do you think I might have known him?"

"I think he was last alive long before you were even a glimmer in your mother's eyes," Skade said softly. "He doesn't remember who he is, either. Did you know that?"

"I had thought you kept him..."

"You thought I did that on purpose," Skade said without rancor. How many other people--Espen included--had thought the same?

"Yes. He *is* your prisoner..."

Skade sighed. "And I am not at all like Terrin."

She tried not to remember how the Ghost had come to be in the mirror in the first place, but it was hard for the memories not to rise up in her mind as she took the vampire's arm and hurried back to her room.

Chapter 20

Alban had been experimenting with the lights again. He had found, with much trial and error, that he could easily manipulate both size and intensity, depending on how great his concentration. He had not tried to do anything else. Lights would do, for now.

He sensed something strange on the horizon; something bad, perhaps, but he could not put his feelings into words that Skade would understand and act upon. His feelings held no shred of proof, no facts. He would no more tell Skade what he felt than he would his father.

But perhaps, he thought, he would speak to the vampire. Surely he, of all people, would be able to decipher Alban's bad feelings, and tell him not to worry.

He truly didn't want to think about anything else. Although he had not been gone from Leysan for a month yet, it felt more like a century. The darkened rooms, the pain of the spell... Alban almost felt as if that had happened to someone else entirely. He didn't feel like a different person; just as if the bad memories were so far into the past that he no longer could remember any details. He began to climb down from his perch on the windowsill, intending to venture out to find the vampire, but he didn't even make it to the door. *Something* erupted in his mind and pulled him down into darkness so swiftly he didn't even have a chance to scream.

In strange, disjointed visions, he saw his father sitting at the head of the council's table, watching calmly as the council members died around him. He watched Terrin's confrontation with Darius, and silently screamed as his own power was used to murder Teluride's friend.

"You did my bidding once, my son, why not do it again?"

Alban tried to deny Terrin the use of his powers. He tried to pull away, to find shelter in some uncharted corner of his mind, but he could not escape from Terrin's quiet laughter.

"You did my bidding once, my son."

"Not willingly," Alban whispered. "I had no idea..."

"And you enjoyed it."

"No..."

"Oh, yes." Alban saw his father now, standing in King Valdis's doorway, a strange little smile on his face. He glanced down when he felt something heavy in his hand, and realized he held the same dagger Terrin had so conveniently found in Teluride's hand.

He heard Skade's voice, as if from far away.

"If you wish, we can always ask my mirror. That way, you'll know for certain whether you are guilty or innocent."

"Guilty or innocent," he whispered, and dropped the dagger.

"Oh, you're definitely guilty," Terrin said softly, and faded from view. "But if you don't believe me, you know what to do."

Alban *did* know what to do. When he opened his eyes and found he lay at the foot of the window, he struggled up and staggered to the door.

He knew what he had to do, and Skade needn't be present to find out if he were guilty or innocent. He would ask the Ghost, and swear him to secrecy if he had to.

He met no one in the hall, and Skade's room was empty, cold, and open to the world. Alban shook his head to clear the blackness from the edges of his vision, and placed one hand on the slick surface of the mirror.

"Are you in there, Ghost?" he whispered, his voice cracking with the effort it cost him to stay awake. What had happened, back in his room? Had he suffered some sort of fit? The swift draining sensation had almost felt like...it had almost felt like Terrin's vanquished spell.

Alban gasped. Had the dreams been sent by Terrin? Was he innocent after all?

Even with this doubt, he knew he would have to make certain of his innocence before he could sleep at all.

"Ghost? Are you in there?"

The Ghost appeared in the mirror, wavering a bit around the edges. He seemed almost hesitant to appear, as if he expected something much worse than Alban.

When he spoke, his voice cracked. "What do you want?"

"I need you to do something for me," Alban said, his hand still pressed against the mirror. "I've been having dreams..."

The Ghost shuddered. "Dreams."

"I need to know who killed my uncle," Alban said. "King Valdis."

The Ghost briefly closed his eyes. When he opened them, he seemed fainter than before, as if the very effort of appearing in the mirror cost him dearly. Belatedly, Alban wondered if there was anything wrong.

"I could..." The Ghost wet his lips. "I could bring out the memory, if you were there, but nothing more than that. If you weren't there, then perhaps Zaira will be able to help."

Alban had heard that name before, but where? Had Skade mentioned it? "Zaira?" he asked aloud.

"She was Terrin's Dreamer," the Ghost whispered, and took a shallow breath. "Keep your hand on the mirror. I'll...do my best to show you what you wish to know."

Alban took a deep breath. "And if I wasn't there, I'd have to ask Zaira?"

The Ghost nodded. He almost seemed to be in pain, but Alban didn't feel confident enough to ask him if anything was wrong. "Are you..."

His voice trailed away when the scene in the mirror abruptly shifted, and he found that he stared at Terrin, with the faint form of the Ghost superimposed over top of him.

"This isn't right," the Ghost whispered. "I did not do this..."

"No, you didn't," Terrin agreed. "*I* did. And I thank you for allowing me to retrieve what is rightfully mine, whoever you are."

Alban saw the Ghost appear in the mirror, and stare at Terrin as if he struggled to place his face in some forgotten memory.

Terrin stared intently at the Ghost for a moment, a frown furrowing his brow. Then he smiled. "I recognize you now."

"You do?" The Ghost sounded as if Terrin had torn those two words from his throat. He vanished briefly, then reappeared, slightly less visible now.

Alban couldn't take his eyes off his father.

"Yes, I recognize you. Do you know me?"

"I know who you are," the Ghost whispered, and Alban thought he tried to back away.

Terrin smiled. "Ah, but do you know who *you* are, Nicodemus?"

The Ghost screamed and vanished, leaving the Mirror open wide to Terrin's desires.

Alban started to take his hand away from the mirror, but it seemed to be stuck fast to the cold glass. He pulled it as hard as he could, fear robbing him of both voice and coherent thought.

Skade's bracelet shimmered on his wrist. Alban stared at it for a moment, struggling to remember what she had told him about it, but the fear overrode everything.

He dimly heard a strange keening noise coming from his throat, and desperately tried to force his voice to a shout.

Terrin laughed at his fright. "Alban, Alban. Did you think I would leave you here in peace when I need you so much in Leysan? Did you think you would never see my again?"

"Let me go..." It cost him a lot to force those words from his throat.

"No. I need you here." Terrin reached out and gently took Alban's hand. "I need your power, Alban."

The spell flared to life in Alban's mind. He knew what it was now, and remembered the tearing pain from before. His only recourse was to fight, even though he knew he could not win against his father's power.

He dug deep down inside his soul, and built a mass of power, keeping it away from the ravages of Terrin's spell. The effort drove deep daggers of pain into his mind, and tore away all hope that he would win free both alive and sane.

Skade's beads blazed into life, casting a bloody glow over the mirror and Terrin's face. Alban took a deep breath, stared into his father's eyes, and threw the gathered power into the only place of contact; their joined hands.

The Mirror shattered, sending shards of glass flying. Alban felt something warm and thick trickle down the front of his face, but he could not find the will to raise his hand to wipe it away. His eyes had closed of their own accord, and he feared he would not have the strength to open them again.

He heard the Ghost scream again from inside his prison, but worse, he heard his father laugh.

"You would be a formidable foe, if you were properly trained," Terrin said. His grip had not been broken by Alban's bid for freedom; in fact Alban's hand burned, as if the burst of power had not quite made it through the contact of their touch.

"Yes, you would have been a formidable foe," Terrin said again, *"if* you had been trained. But you were not."

Dazed and aching, Alban did not struggle as his father began to pull him into the mirror. He tried to pull away, but the bolt of pain that streaked down his arm at the movement almost cost him his tenuous hold on consciousness. He couldn't hear the Ghost screaming anymore. *Had he killed Skade's prisoner?* He didn't have the strength to find out.

"What is going on?" A new voice intruded upon Alban's ears, its bell-like tones shaking him out of his daze. He raised his head, and found he stared at Skade and the vampire from the other side of ruined mirror now. Terrin had managed to pull him through it, but he had to close the portal he had made. One more second, and Alban would be lost in Leysan, too far away from Skade's magic for her to be of use to him ever again.

"I'm taking back what is rightly mine," Terrin said, unperturbed. "You might want to check on your Mirror's health; I'm afraid my son's bid for freedom might have hurt him quite badly."

"Let Alban go," the vampire said, starting forward. Alban flung out one hand, intending to grip the edge of the mirror and pull himself out, and the vampire clutched his hand. "Alban, fight him!"

"Alban," Terrin said softly. "Let go of the mirror and come with me."

Alban felt his fingers loosen even as he struggled to make them stay. The vampire, at least, seemed to know what had happened. With one glance back at Skade, who stood rigid in the doorway, the vampire lunged for Alban's hand.

As Skade grabbed for the vampire, her bracelet slipped from Alban's wrist. He felt his bloodslicked hand slip from the vampire's grip a second later, and could only watch in horror as Terrin blocked whatever magic Skade flung at him, and took the vampire as well.

He had no more strength to fight. As the mirror portal shimmered and began to close; as Skade's white face began to fade from both sight and memory, Alban let the darkness carry him away into oblivion.

It was over almost before she had a chance to act. Skade had sensed something wrong as soon as she and the vampire approached her room, but she had expected the Ghost to be the cause of the feeling, not Terrin.

She had not expected him at all.

How had he broken through her spells and wards? How had he gotten Alban to...

She had told him the Ghost might be able to find out if he was guilty or innocent. Skade groaned. She had told him, and he had decided not to wait for her to act.

She walked up to the shattered mirror, and saw the faint shimmer of her spell, the only thing still keeping the Ghost in his prison.

"Mirror? Are you..."

A faint moan reached her ears. Without a thought to safety, Skade stepped through the mirror's frame and into that gray, featureless place again, the Ghost's prison, now swarming with the echo of both pain and fear.

"Are you okay?" She couldn't see him, but she sensed he was near. Near enough to hear her? She sent out a thin tendril of magic, but he eluded her grasp.

"I..." His voice cracked. He almost sounded as if he were crying. "I know who I am."

That had been the cause of the surge through her magical protections. Espen had warned her that this might happen, but Skade had not listened. As usual, she had discounted Espen's irritating wisdom, and gone about her business without a care to anyone's safety.

"I see," she said, and wondered if he were strong enough to attack her here. She thought not, but it wouldn't hurt to be cautious nonetheless.

"I...I know my name. I know what I did to become your prisoner."

Something shimmered in the air in front of her. Skade held out her hand.

"Why don't you come with me, and we can discuss it somewhere safer?" she asked, keeping her voice calm. *He knew his name. Had he truly remembered everything?* His name, the horrible thing her son, Terrin, and this confused prophet had done...

And Terrin had been the one breaking through the mirror.

"Did you help Terrin steal them?" Skade snapped. "Did you help him, Nicodemus?" Since he had said he knew his name, she saw no reason to hide it any longer. *What would Espen say when she discovered what had happened?*

The ghostly smear in the air before her jerked back when she named him. He shimmered into being, haggard and pale, his eyes seeking escape even as he stood in front of her.

"Nicodemus," she spoke his name without anger now. She couldn't believe he had helped Terrin, even inadvertently. "What happened?"

He flinched again, as if the speaking of his name caused him a bit more than physical pain. Terrin's spell had caused him pain before, she remembered. But he had recovered from that.

"What happened, Nicodemus?" she asked once more. "If you won't tell me, I can force you to. I don't want to do that, but..."

"Alban came here," the Ghost whispered. His voice shook with weariness, but she couldn't afford to let him sleep yet. "He said he wanted to know for certain if he had killed his uncle. I said..." he took a wavering breath and closed his eyes. "I said if he was in the room at the time, I could find out. But I didn't have a chance..."

"What happened when you tried to show him?" Skade asked. She felt her spell begin to unravel now that it did not have the mirror to anchor it, and pulled it back with a thought.

"T-Terrin appeared..." The Ghost sank to his knees. "He...he knew my name."

So it hadn't been a natural remembrance. Skade was oddly relieved, although she suspected Terrin had hammered at the wall Nicodemus had built around his mind with much less finesse than she would have herself.

"I didn't help him," he sobbed. "I didn't help him..."

Skade wanted to wipe the entire kingdom of Leysan off the face of the map, but she kept a tight reign on her temper, and tried not to let it bleed through into her voice. She needed Nicodemus, now that he had regained his memories. The alternative was Zaira, but Skade didn't want to admit her failure to Espen just yet.

She had lost both Alban and the vampire, something she could not dismiss lightly. And Terrin had been asking for trouble for fifteen years, ever since he had abandoned his 'friends' to their fates.

"Listen to me." She waited until his sobs had tapered off enough for her to know he was listening. "I didn't put you under a single spell, Nicodemus. I have not mistreated you, have I?"

He flinched at his name, and mutely shook his head.

Skade took a deep breath. She was angry enough at Terrin to botch this attempt at diplomacy with a ghost young enough and confused enough to do something stupid with his newfound knowledge, but she needed his help. She could not afford to alienate him.

"I need your help to get them back."

He stared up at her, fear warring with interest in his eyes. "But Terrin..."

"However much Terrin might want to believe it, he is not all-knowing," Skade said sharply. "He is not all-powerful, either."

Nicodemus didn't reply to that, but huddled in a ball on the floor, his arms pressed tightly against his chest.

Skade stared at him for a moment. "If you help me, I'll let you keep your name. That's the least I can do."

He stared up at her, obviously not believing her words. "You'll let me keep my name?"

"Yes." What else could she offer? He couldn't ever be freed, and she didn't think he'd be satisfied with a bigger mirror or an explanation as to why she had treated him the way she had so long ago.

"What do you need me to do?" he finally asked. His breath hitched in his throat when he spoke, and she thought he might begin to cry.

"I need to get into Leysan to rescue Alban and the vampire," Skade said softly. "Alban and his brother." She shook her head. "I should have seen that..."

"The vampire is Alban's brother?" Nicodemus asked, forgetting his fear of her in the face of curiosity.

"He did everything but tell me outright," Skade said, still not able to believe she had not figured that out from the beginning. "He even said Terrin couldn't siphon power from anyone not related to him. And I didn't see it."

The Ghost took a deep breath. "I'll need a new mirror," he whispered, not trusting himself to meet her gaze.

"I have plenty of mirrors," Skade sighed. She held out her hand again. "Will you come with me?"

Nicodemus hesitated, then placed his hand in hers. Again, she marveled that he had any solidity at all, being a ghost.

And an hour later, after removing the shattered mirror and hanging another one in its place, she discovered that rescuing Alban and the vampire from Leysan might be a bit more difficult than she had expected, since Terrin was using all of his power to prevent her from reaching his son.

With stolen power, Terrin locked Leysan's castle away from prying eyes; locked it so tightly that Alban's ears rang with the repercussions.

Alban stared up at his father with a heavy rock of dread in his chest, closing off all ability to flee. The vampire seemed to be similarly frozen. Alban saw him huddled against the wall not far away, his eyes glittering in the wash of light from Terrin's magic.

Skade would never reach them now. Alban felt his last ray of hope shrivel in his chest at the thought of being trapped in Leysan with his father, for however long Terrin let him live. And what about the vampire?

"For the first time in my life, I have everything I've ever wanted under one roof," Terrin said, and turned away from spellcasting to regard his prisoners. "My sons, my rightful crown." He smiled down at Alban. "What more could I ask for?"

"Your *sons*?" Alban asked, his voice cracking with the effort to speak. He glanced at the vampire, who shifted uncomfortably under his gaze.

Terrin laughed. "Yes. My *sons*. Twins, actually, but you'd never guess it, now."

Indeed, Alban would never have guessed the vampire was his brother, much less his twin.

"You're my brother?" He ignored his father in place of the vampire, who cast a frightened look at Terrin before replying.

"Yes. I'm your brother."

"And you knew all this time and didn't tell me?"

With another sidelong glance at Terrin, the vampire seemed to expect to be struck down where he sat.

"I couldn't tell you," he finally whispered.

"No, he couldn't," Terrin agreed. "I wouldn't let him."

The vampire closed his eyes. Alban noticed that one of his hands was closed in a fist against his chest, but he couldn't imagine what the vampire might be hiding.

"Stand up," Terrin said mildly. Alban felt power behind his words; power that belied his apparent calmness.

The vampire stayed where he was, his eyes still closed, a small figure against the backdrop of Leysan's throneroom.

Alban struggled to sit up, and felt something hot and wet slip down over his lips. He put his hand to his nose, and it came away covered with blood. His other hand was burned and blackened from his previous attempt at freedom.

"Stand up," Terrin ordered again.

Alban felt nothing, so he presumed the order had to be for the vampire. But why wouldn't he stand up? Did he *want* Terrin to be angry?

He tried to get to his feet, and swayed dizzily for a moment before finding himself on the floor again, too weakened by Terrin's spell to stand.

This time, there would be no ghostly apparition to offer them a chance at freedom. This time, there would be no mirror magic to save them.

This time, he thought he might die before he managed to escape.

"Stand up," Terrin said. Alban sensed a curious sort of finality in his voice, as if he was willing to give the vampire one last chance to obey.

The vampire opened his eyes and stared straight at Terrin.

"No." His voice hardly shook at all when he said this, and Alban marveled at his bravery.

Terrin sat very still on his ill-gotten throne. "What did you say?"

"I said no," the vampire whispered. "You don't own me anymore, Terrin. You can't force me to do your bidding, ever again."

Terrin laughed. Evidently, laughter was not what the vampire expected. He glanced uneasily at Alban, but Alban had no strength left to give him any assurances.

"But *I* know your name," he said. "I know who you are. And if I break that last spell, *vampire*, you'll wish you had done my bidding one last time."

The vampire stood. Alban faded out for a minute there, and when he could see again, the vampire had reached Terrin's throne.

When Terrin reached out to touch him, Alban tried to get to his feet to warn him away, but it was too late.

An arc of pure power sprang from Terrin's fingertips and vanished into the vampire's body, fueled by Alban's own power.

"What are you doing?" Alban asked hoarsely, waiting for the vampire to fall. His thin form seemed to be wracked with shivers now, or convulsions, but he stayed on his feet. Alban could only marvel at his courage.

He noticed that the vampire's hand was still clenched. Was that a glint of red shining from his fingers? Alban knew he should know what that red glow meant, but his mind had no patience for puzzles.

Terrin drew on the spell again, and sent another bolt of power into the vampire's body. This time, he crumpled to his knees.

"Stop," Alban whispered, struggling to his feet. "Stop hurting him!"

"'Stop hurting him!'" Terrin mocked. "He is mine, Alban, to do with as I wish."

The vampire crouched low on the floor, his eyes squeezed shut so tightly that blood leaked out from beneath his eyelids.

"Please," Alban whispered. He tried to find the strength to rise and stop his father, but he couldn't seem to force his legs to hold him. He dragged himself over to where the vampire cowered, one hand outstretched to give what little comfort he could.

Before Alban could touch him, Terrin grabbed the front of the vampire's shirt and hauled him upright. "What are you hiding? What do you have in your hands?"

The vampire gave Alban a look he could not decipher, and let his hand fall open.

Like liquid fire, the ring of Skade's beads spilled out onto the floor. Alban lunged for them, scraping his wounded hand across the floor in clumsy haste.

Terrin stepped on his hand before he could close his stiff fingers around the beads. Alban almost screamed from the pain. He swallowed the scream, barely, and stared up at his father with tear-blurred eyes.

"Let us go..." It even hurt to breathe now, with his hand throbbing, and the spell throwing everything else awry. Alban tried to pull his hand away, but a white-hot burst of pain left him writhing on the floor. He had no idea if the pain came from the spell or from the burns, and he had no desire to try it again to find out.

"Why would I want to let you go?" Terrin asked. "I have what I want-- your power--and I'm not about to give that up now."

Alban slumped back against the floor, releasing the beads. Terrin finally lifted his foot and dropped the vampire, who fell to the floor, his eyes closed.

Terrin turned away. "Gather your strength," he told Alban, "We're going to seal the castle even tighter. I don't want to lose you again."

Before Alban could protest that he didn't have enough power left to do even the simplest of tasks, he felt the spell erupt in his mind, driving him downward into darkness too thick to pierce.

Chapter 21

The vampire lay on the floor for a little while, content to be forgotten. He didn't think he was dying. Terrin's bolts of power were painful, but not life-threatening.

Not for him.

Alban, on the other hand, was haggard and pale, his face gray with exhaustion. He had folded up without a sound as soon as Terrin activated the spell again, and the vampire had anxiously waited for him to start breathing when the spell had stolen the very breath from his body.

A full minute after Terrin left the room, he had, but the vampire didn't think he would last much longer. Terrin would kill him, and then what?

To utilize the vampire's powers again, Terrin would have to release him from the spell and give him back his name.

And he had never been very powerful, by Terrin's exacting standards. He remembered that much, at least.

Alban coughed. Bright blood trickled out of the side of his mouth, joining the drying blood that had poured out of his nose early on. His burned hand--the product of his attempt at freedom--lay curled on his chest.

For what seemed to be the longest time, the vampire sat and watched him breathe. He couldn't think to do anything else.

And when he felt the spell rise up again to smother Alban, he watched in silence as Alban's breath faltered, then stopped. When Terrin stormed into the room a moment later, the vampire couldn't even find enough room past the pain for grief.

Alone in Skade's rooms for the first time in weeks, the Ghost sat inside his new Mirror and tried to worm his way inside Terrin's defenses to see if Alban and the vampire still lived.

He had not thought much about the knowledge he now possessed; indeed, he preferred not to think about it at all. The long-ago chain of events that had ended with him a prisoner in Skade's mirror could no longer affect him, save for the first shock of memory.

He wondered, carefully, lest the wonderings loose something hidden in his mind, what had happened to Skade's son, Michael. On the tail end of that thought was the realization that he would never ask Skade herself; he didn't dare. The cocky, vain young prophet who would have demanded to know had died fifteen years ago. Nicodemus could only work with what was left.

He tried his best to find a way past Terrin's defenses, but the entire castle seemed to be locked tight, giving him no room to maneuver between the layers of Terrin's spells. He kept trying, though, unwilling to give up until Skade ordered him to stop.

He thought he might continue even then. He had liked the vampire and felt sorry for Alban. He would hate to see them die because he did not try hard enough to save them.

Unless... Skade *had* mentioned giving Alban a bracelet; a direct link to her power. Not many wizards used vessels to store power in anymore, but Skade was one of the old school; a product of a bygone age, no matter how young she appeared.

Technically, she should have been able to call to that bracelet and magically enter the castle then. Had she tried it already and failed?

Instead of searching for a way inside, the Ghost now searched for the telltale signature of Skade's distinct magic.

He found it on his second try.

If he closed his eyes and focused, he found he could send a tendril of himself into the room where the bracelet *was*, although he could not see a thing. He placed that tendril of himself inside the bracelet, coaxing the dormant power to waken until he could hear a furious conversation somewhere overhead.

Where was the bracelet? Almost without realizing it, Nicodemus projected both darkened scene and conversation onto the surface of his mirror in the hope that Skade would walk into her room and discover what he had found. He didn't dare to open his eyes or try to contact her in any way; the contact with the bracelet in Leysan was tenuous at best. He could very easily lose it.

He concentrated on the conversation and tried to glean any references to Alban or the vampire.

"...dead?" he heard Terrin asked. "He can't be. I didn't take *that* much power from him."

Nicodemus heard something shift above the beads, and a glimmer of light appeared. Someone--he supposed it was the vampire, although he had no proof of that yet--lay on top of Skade's bracelet.

Nicodemus fed power into the bracelet until he heard the vampire gasp, then saw him shift away.

His view of things was skewed and ungainly from inside the confines of one of the beads, but Nicodemus recognized Alban, lying silent and still on the floor not far away. The vampire's face loomed down at him. His eyes were dazed, and full of grief and pain.

"Alban's dead," he whispered, whether for Nicodemus' benefit or Terrin's, the Ghost did not know.

"You've told me that before," Nicodemus heard Terrin say above him. "I don't believe you."

"He's not breathing," the vampire pointed out.

This was true. Even Nicodemus could see that much.

"He can't be dead," Terrin repeated, shaking his son. Alban did not respond. Indeed, he looked even paler now, as if disturbing him had only made the situation worse.

"You might need to give him some of your power to save his life," the vampire whispered, and struggled to sit up. He made sure the bracelet was safely hidden under his hand, but enough space appeared through his fingers for Nicodemus to watch.

"I'm not giving him any power," Terrin growled, and shook Alban again.

"You did the same with me, didn't you?" the vampire asked, as if the thought had just occurred to him. "You drained me dry. That's why I'm like...this, isn't it?"

Terrin smiled. "What makes you think that?" he asked. "And what makes you think that I can't break that one last spell, and drain you just as you claim I've drained Alban?"

"He isn't breathing," the vampire said again. His voice shook with weariness.

"Neither are you," Terrin snapped. "Wake him up." He kicked Alban's body over to where the vampire sat. Nicodemus had no idea what he expected to solve by doing that, but it seemed to make Terrin happier.

The vampire's hand clenched suddenly around the beads. Nicodemus thought he knew why; Alban's face was covered with drying blood, and the vampire was obviously weak and in pain.

Could Skade help them? If he broke the connection now and tried to find her, would she get mad at him for breaking the connection, or would she be happy that he had found a way to get inside Leysan? He knew he could not help them; he had no substance even when he could enter places without the use of her magic. He also had no way to assure the vampire that he would return. He had no way to tell the vampire he was really there.

Nicodemus closed his eyes. *What should he do?* Waiting for Skade would solve nothing; he feared he would have to break the contact anyway to speak to her.

As carefully as he could, he eased away from the bracelet, leaving a tiny thread of awareness inside one bead. The effort was almost too exhausting to bear, but he managed to get back to his mirror with only a minimum of difficulty.

Skade still wasn't in her room, and he had no true idea how to find her. He would have to check every mirror in Iomar, plus every reflective surface he could find to track down his Queen before it was too late.

And he had a feeling that time was running out.

Chapter 22

Finally, Terrin seemed to realize that Alban was truly dead. He stood for a moment, staring down at his son, then turned his gaze to the vampire.

"You can bring him back to life."

The vampire was already weakened. He had passed through hunger and come out on the other side, dangerously weak and lightheaded, but sane enough.

"Bring him back to life? How?" And then, suddenly, the vampire knew. "No."

"You'd defy me?" Terrin asked softly.

The vampire tried not to stare at the blood drying on Alban's face. "No." He would never wish his existence on *anyone*, especially Alban.

His brother.

Terrin unsheathed a small dagger and placed it against Alban's neck. "I don't think you'd be able to help yourself if I cut his throat. Tell me the truth. Would you?"

The vampire licked his lips. His face felt numb, almost as if Terrin had forced him to drink poison. He closed his eyes. "No."

The sharp, sweet smell of blood permeated the air. When the vampire opened his eyes, Terrin slid the dagger back into his belt and motioned to Alban.

"Save his life."

The room slowly started to swing around his head. He swayed, dizzy and sick. Blood slipped down the side of Alban's throat.

"Do it," Terrin ordered gently.

With a strangled groan, the vampire bent to drink.

Nicodemus found his Queen seated in her garden, a rose in one hand and tears on her cheeks. He watched her for a moment from the shelter of an algae-laden pool. Did he dare disturb her? If he waited until she returned to her rooms, both Alban and the vampire could very well be dead by then.

"My Queen?"

Skade dropped the rose and quickly wiped the tears away. Nicodemus saw the old anger appear in her eyes when she realized who had spoken, and he tried to quench the fear that accompanied her anger. He would be able to save them and be frightened of Skade at the same time.

"I managed to see into Leysan, my Queen," he said to forestall any punishment for disturbing her. "The bracelet you gave Alban..."

He watched her try to decide whether to punish him or not, but only relaxed when she summoned up a smile.

"I'm not going to hurt you, Nicodemus," she said. "Tell me what happened."

The algae would not be conductive to showing her what he had seen.

"I would suggest we return to your room, my Lady," he ventured. "I can't show you much with fish swimming across my..."

He stuttered to a stop at the expression on her face.

"Did you just make a *joke*?" she asked suspiciously. When he couldn't find any words to reply, she waved her question away. "You're right, of course. Meet me back at my Mirror, and show me what you discovered."

Five minutes later, Skade arrived at the door, a little out of breath from the rush.

"What did you find?"

Nicodemus showed her. She was silent for a long time after that, her eyes shiny with tears again.

"I had hoped you could use the power in the bracelet to rescue them," Nicodemus said. "If Alban is still alive."

"You couldn't tell?"

"He wasn't breathing, but Terrin might know of a way to revive him. I don't know." For the first time since he regained his memories, Nicodemus felt a twinge of sympathy for Skade. He thought he knew how she felt, watching on the sidelines unable to help.

"I wish I could do something for them," he whispered, remembering the look on the vampire's face.

"You can do one thing," Skade whispered, and bowed her head. "Call Espen. I can't put it off any longer. She has to know."

Then she had given up. Nicodemus banished the scene from the mirror, and with a heavy heart went to do her bidding.

Chapter 23

Alban opened his eyes and found he lay at the foot of Terrin's throne. The stone floor beneath him froze the marrow in his bones and made his head ache.

"It worked."

Alban intuitively knew that his father was speaking softly, but his voice somehow reverberated through his head, making it pound even worse than before. He groaned and tried to turn away from the sound.

"Yes." This voice was paper-thin and torn with weariness, as if the speaker had no strength left for speech.

"I don't need you anymore, then, do I?"

Terrin walked into Alban's line of vision, then right out again, ignoring him completely.

Alban turned his head enough to see who the other voice belonged to. He saw the vampire lying a few feet away from the throne, so shrunken and still that Alban assumed he was dead.

But if he were dead, how had he spoken? And what had Terrin done to him? He wet his lips and tasted blood. What had happened? The last thing he remembered was darkness washing over everything as Terrin activated the spell again. He had felt something tug at his heart, then nothing. Had he died?

He managed to roll over, and the vampire raised his head enough to stare.

"I don't need you anymore," Terrin said again. "And it seems to be a bit difficult to kill you, so I guess you'll have to spend the rest of your life in the dungeons."

The vampire didn't reply to that. Alban noticed that he had one hand clenched up against his chest, but he couldn't remember what that meant or why it should matter.

His own hand didn't hurt anymore. Alban stared at it and found it smooth and unburned. Hadn't it been aching and blistered before?

His mind did not want to struggle with the problem. It slid away into darkness where the rest of his problems lay.

"What are you going to do with Alban?" the vampire whispered.

Terrin glanced back at Alban, who lay as still as he could, trying to pretend he had not moved. The first worm of fear burrowed into his chest.

"Alban will serve me until I don't need him anymore," Terrin said. "I see no reason why he cannot serve me forever, Alexander."

He said the vampire's name so casually that Alban didn't notice at first, but the vampire did.

A medley of emotions crossed his face, from shock to dazed acceptance in the space of a few seconds.

Terrin reached down and placed one hand on his heart before he could grapple with the knowledge of his name and what that entailed.

Alban felt the spell surge into life. The vampire--Alexander--screamed. And when darkness bloomed in his mind, he was only too glad to embrace it and let it carry him away.

You can find ALL our books up on our website at:

http://www.writers-exchange.com

All Jennifer's books:

http://www.writers-exchange.com/Jennifer-St-Clair/

all our fantasy novels:

http://www.writers-exchange.com/category/genres/fantasy/

About the Author

Jennifer St. Clair grew up in Southern Ohio and spent most of her childhood in the woods around her home. She wrote her first novel when she was thirteen, and hasn't stopped since. She lives with her ball python, Fester, and two cats, Ash and Rowan.

In her spare time, she crochets, makes cloth dolls, collects antiques, books, and vintage clothing, and takes digital photographs with varying degrees of success.

Her *Beth-Hill series* is set in the area in America that contains many supernatural creatures: Wild Hunt, Vampires, Dragons, Faery and more.

It is part of the Universe that her *Jacob Lane Series, Karen Montgomery Series* and vampire trilogy, *The Shadow Series* are set in.

Follow all her books on her author page:

http://www.writers-exchange.com/Jennifer-St-Clair/

If you want to read more about other books by this author, they are listed on the following pages...

A Beth-Hill Novel (Stand Alone Novels)

Are creatures of the night and all manner of extramundane beings drawn to certain locations in the natural world? In the Midwestern village of Beth-Hill located in southern Ohio, the population is made up of its fair share of common citizens...and much more than its share of supernatural residents. Take a walk on the wild side in this unusual place where imagination meets reality.

Blood of Innocents

Ten years ago, Orien, crown prince of the Seleighe, was captured by his mortal enemies, locked in a dungeon and turned into a vampire. Six years into Orien's sentence, the Healer's brother Cullen disobeyed his mistress's orders to kill him and turned him into a vampire instead, thus sealing both their fates for all eternity.

Now both Orien and Cullen are set free. But a secret only Cullen knows lies locked inside his mind, threatening to drive him mad before he can uncover the identity of a traitor--the very elf who betrayed Orien and left them both to die in darkness.

Publisher: http://www.writers-exchange.com/blood-of-innocents/

Full Moon

Werewolves change into wolves when the moon is full. But Edward's curse only allows him to be *human* when the moon is full.

Alone and despairing, Edward hides himself away from the world. He's scraped out a meager existence for himself for almost a century in the forest he's grown to love and call home. But in the depths of a terrible winter, he stumbles across clues from the life his mother left behind in Faerie. The truth may give him the answers he needs about the source of his birthright... and the curse that holds him captive.

Publisher: http://www.writers-exchange.com/full-moon/

A Beth-Hill Novel: Jacob Lane Series

Are creatures of the night and all manner of extramundane beings drawn to certain locations in the natural world? In the Midwestern village of Beth-Hill located in southern Ohio, the population is made up of its fair share of common citizens...and much more than its share of supernatural residents.

Jacob Lane is a ten-year-old girl who's spent her life unaware of her magical heritage. After being sent to Darkbrook, a school of magic, supernatural mysteries seem to spring to life all around her and her new friends.

Book 1: The Tenth Ghost

After Jacob Lane's parents mysteriously vanish, she's sent to Darkbrook, the only school of magic in the United States. While there, she and her new friends stumble upon a series of mysterious deaths in the nine ghosts that haunt the halls of Darkbrook. These ghosts were students who died at the school over the past hundred years. Will Jacob become the tenth ghost, or can she stop a witch's reign of terror?

Publisher: http://www.writers-exchange.com/the-tenth-ghost/

Book 2: The Ninth Guest

When Jacob's friend Ophelia's family decides to open up their castle for guests, amateur paranormal sleuth Jacob Lane is invited to join in on the fun. "Spend the night in a vampire's castle and live to tell the tale!" is supposed to be a fundraiser to help Ophelia's family pay the bills. Heating a castle costs quite a bit, after all. But, after the truth of an old secret is uncovered, what began as an innocent business venture soon turns deadly when vampire hunters get involved.

For years, the vampire hunters have had only one goal: To destroy all vampires. With the help of a new friend, Jacob and Ophelia must work together to save the entire VonBriggle family from extinction.

Publisher: http://www.writers-exchange.com/the-ninth-guest/

Book 3: The Eighth Room

For two hundred years, the Selkies have kept themselves separate from those who live on land. But now the Selkies need allies or they'll be crushed by their ancient enemies, the Finfolk.

Jacob and Ophelia, students at the only school of magic in the United States, uncover a mystery that dates back to Darkbrook's beginnings. While helping clean out old storage rooms for classroom expansion, they find something that might save the Selkies from extinction. With the help of the youngest member of the Wild Hunt who are no longer so wild or terrifying, they must foil the Finfolk who desire the Selkie's destruction...or die trying.

Publisher: http://www.writers-exchange.com/the-eighth-room/

Book 4: The Seventh Secret

After a picture of Niklas, the dragons' liaison to the only school of magic in the United States, shows up in too many newspapers to count, Darkbrook is forced to go on the defensive. The secret of Darkbrook's existence has been discovered. But there are more than dragonhunters in the forest, and, as Jacob Lane, supernatural sleuth and student at Darkbrook, learns how to use her newly discovered talent of healing, she helps to right an old wrong and must battle a teenaged wizard intent on proving--once and for all--that magic is real.

Publisher: http://www.writers-exchange.com/the-seventh-secret/

Book 5: The Sixth Stone

Jacob Lane, supernatural sleuth, and Danny, her werewolf friend, stumble across an alternate world where the Wild Hunt was never bound, and Darkbrook, the school of magic they attend, was abandoned a hundred years ago.

But when the Hounds of the Hunt wish to surrender, the two students are swept up in a whirlwind of heartbreak, betrayal, and the discovery of a lost treasure.

Publisher: http://www.writers-exchange.com/the-sixth-stone/

A Beth-Hill Novella: Karen Montgomery Series

Are creatures of the night and all manner of extramundane beings drawn to certain locations in the natural world? In the Midwestern village of Beth-Hill located in southern Ohio, the population is made up of its fair share of common citizens...and much more than its share of supernatural residents. Take a walk on the wild side in this unusual place where imagination meets reality.

Karen Montgomery was an ordinary woman until she stumbled into the extraordinary... A bargain with elves worth its weight in gold. A plague of sinister ladybugs. Rogue vampire hunters, including one who tries to turn over a new leaf--with disastrous consequences. A ghostly huntsmen of the Wild Hunt wishing for redemption. Karen's life will never be the same again.

Book 1: Budget Cuts

Karen Montgomery is used to taking care of the unpleasant jobs no one else wants to deal with. When a shortage of funds forces her to fire fifteen employees from the library, she isn't happy, but the nasty task has to be done and she is, after all, the boss. But Karen finds finishing her task impossible when she can't seem to track down Ivy Bedinghaus, a night clerk she's never actually met. Once she finally does confront Ivy, she's thrust into a centuries-old conflict that makes her previous troubles radically pale in comparison.

Publisher: http://www.writers-exchange.com/budget-cuts/

Book 2: The Secret of Redemption

Karen Montgomery, librarian, finds herself embroiled in another otherworldly adventure...

A member of the Wild Hunt--ghostly myths that aren't so ghostly (or myth-like) anymore--needs help in reconciling who he once was in life and who he is now.

A little girl has gone missing. And the one most likely responsible for her disappearance is the one Karen must prove innocent.

Publisher: http://www.writers-exchange.com/the-secret-of-redemption/

Book 3: Ladybug, Ladybug

An innocent attempt to rid the library of a plague of ladybugs turns sinister when a rogue vampire hunter gets the contract for pest control.

Ivy Bedinghaus, who works for Karen as a night clerk--along with all the vampires in Beth-Hill--are in danger, and their only hope for survival is with the help of Karen, a member of the Wild Hunt, and Russell Moore, a reformed vampire hunter.

Publisher: http://www.writers-exchange.com/ladybug-ladybug/

Book 4: Detour

One wrong turn sends Karen down a road that shouldn't exist, to the site of an old accident and an even older mystery. With reformed vampire hunter Russell Moore's help, Karen finds the key to the mystery. But Russ keeps his own secrets...some of which are deadly.

When old friends from Russ' past come to call, Karen realizes his secrets might just mean his doom. After a terrible incident three years ago, before Karen met him, Russ wants only to live the rest of his life quietly in Beth-Hill. But his secret might not allow him the new lease on life Russ longs for.

Publisher: http://www.writers-exchange.com/detour/

Companion Story: Russ' Story: Capture

Long before Russell Moore ever met supernatural sleuth Karen Montgomery or set foot in Beth-Hill, he was a vampire hunter, possibly the best vampire hunter of all. He brought down whole nests of vampires, caring little about the consequences of his actions. Anyone who lived with or helped the vampires became enemies to be slaughtered.

So what kind of an idiot would capture a ruthless vampire hunter without a conscience and try to reform him?

Ethan Walker was that idiot. Wanting to protect his family, Ethan set out to prove to Russ that vampires weren't all evil, soulless creatures. If Russ would allow himself to witness their lives, see their humanity, surely he and other vampire hunters like him would let them live in peace. *Surely?*

Publisher: http://www.writers-exchange.com/capture/

Secrets When in Shadow Lie

Twelve years ago, Ryan Grey was cursed by a witch to hide a secret. He's lived with the curse of being unable to die permanently, and, over the years he's slowly losing the memory of his past until almost nothing remains.

But now, after a chance meeting with an elf named Zipporah, he discovers the key to unlocking the secret and breaking the curse once and for all...if he can survive the breaking.

Publisher: http://www.writers-exchange.com/secrets-when-in-shadow-lie/

The Dead Who Do Not Sleep

Will Spark only wants a good night's sleep after a night of drinking. Instead, two thugs bang on his door, demanding answers to questions he can't understand. And then they killed him...

Publisher: http://www.writers-exchange.com/the-dead-who-do-not-sleep/

A Beth-Hill Novel: The Abby Duncan Series

Are creatures of the night and all manner of extramundane beings drawn to certain locations in the natural world? In the Midwestern village of Beth-Hill located in southern Ohio, the population is made up of its fair share of common citizens...and much more than its share of supernatural residents. Take a walk on the wild side in this unusual place where imagination meets reality.

Situated in Beth-Hill, where imagination meets reality, is The Rose Emporium, owned by elderly and not-a-little-odd Rose Duncan. The large Victorian house smackdab in the middle of nowhere is a cross between a pawn shop and an antique store that caters to supernatural creatures needing to barter. Rose's twenty-something niece, Abby Duncan, discovers that the world isn't made up of just run-of-the-mill, ordinary humans but an entire spectrum of unusual beings. With her preconceptions about what's normal and what's not turned upside-down, Abby is in for a whole lot of startling truths, mysteries-- about herself and the people and places around her--and danger.

Novella 1: By Any Other Name

Woodturner Abby Duncan decides to sell her spindles at a local Renaissance Festival with only some success. After all, no one really spins their own yarn anymore, do they? While there, she discovers that one of her newfound friends is not what he appears--and his secret is about to get him killed!

Publisher: http://www.writers-exchange.com/by-any-other-name/

Book 2: The Uncrowned Queen

Abby Duncan's elderly Aunt Rose has always been a bit odd. And now she's off on a mysterious trip, leaving Abby behind to run the Rose Emporium, an unusual sort of antique shop. Such an extraordinary store would have been a perfect place for Seth and the others, her friends from the Renaissance Festival, to take a break from traveling between Faires. But when tragedy strikes and Abby and the others discover the true nature of the Rose Emporium, they'll have to travel into Faerie itself before their tightknit group is whole again.

Abby doesn't know much about her family history, but she's about to find out the truth...whether she likes it or not.

Publisher: http://www.writers-exchange.com/the-uncrowned-queen/

Book 3: Coming Soon!

A Beth-Hill Novel: The Shadows Trilogy

Are creatures of the night and all manner of extramundane beings drawn to certain locations in the natural world? In the Midwestern village of Beth-Hill located in southern Ohio, the population is made up of its fair share of common citizens...and much more than its share of supernatural residents. Take a walk on the wild side in this unusual place where imagination meets reality.

A Dreamer dreams the future when the past is not yet laid to rest. Ten years ago, a plague swept across the Seven Kingdoms. Ten years ago, the Queen of Iomar's son was exiled and named the author of the magical plague. Now, in the present, Terrin works to complete his ultimate goal: Control of the Seven Kingdoms using his son's power to supplement his own. But his attempt at dominion meets resistance and the fate of the world rests in the unlikely hands of an exiled prince, a Dreamer, and a vampire...

Book 1: The Prince of Shadows

When Alban's father Terrin appeared at the castle door with a vampire in tow and apologies on his lips, Alban fell under his spell just like everyone else and welcomed him home. But Terrin didn't return to live quietly in his brother's kingdom. He had other plans and, with Alban's untrained powers at his disposal, he begins his ruthless plan to destroy the Seven Kingdoms and rule them all, beginning with his brother's death.

Terrin engineers events to cast the blame on his nephew, Teluride, intending to see the boy executed for his father's murder. But there are those who would thwart Terrin in his mad plan for power, and Alban forms an unlikely alliance with Skade, the reclusive Queen of Iomar, and Terrin's slave, a young vampire with no memory of his name or origins. Although the future looks grim, Alban and the vampire attempt to stop Terrin...and they almost succeed.

A darker history lies at the heart of Terrin's treachery, and only Skade knows the true reason why Terrin would murder his own brother and attempt to destroy both Alban and the vampire to achieve his goals. The Ghost who resides in Skade's mirror--her servant and thrall--holds one of the keys to Terrin's madness. Unfortunately, more than one person wishes for the past to remain the past and the future to hold no shadows of what might have been...

Publisher: http://www.writers-exchange.com/the-prince-of-shadows/

Book 2: Lost In Shadows

Events set in motion ten years ago come to a head as Skade, the reclusive Queen of Iomar, and Nicodemus, who is imprisoned by Skade, struggle to free Alban and the vampire from Terrin's grasp. Old secrets come to light when Skade's exiled son is forced to face his past--or die trying to redeem himself once and for all. Can the crimes of the past truly be forgiven? Only time will tell...and time is running out.

Publisher: http://www.writers-exchange.com/lost-in-shadows/

Book 3: Bound In Shadows

With his power crushed, brother to the king and father to Alban, Terrin is forced to take drastic measures to regain his sons after they are freed and harness the power they possess. But he has an ally inside the healer's house where they are recovering who works to further his plans. The Queen of Iomar, Skade's son, courts redemption to try to save his mother's life, and the vampire who no longer remembers his own name dreams a dream that might save them all...or damn them if success is thwarted.

Publisher: http://www.writers-exchange.com/bound-in-shadows/

A Beth-Hill Novel: Wild Hunt Series

Are creatures of the night and all manner of extramundane beings drawn to certain locations in the natural world? In the Midwestern village of Beth-Hill located in southern Ohio, the population is made up of its fair share of common citizens...and much more than its share of supernatural residents. Take a walk on the wild side in this unusual place where imagination meets reality.

The Wild Hunt roamed the forest outside of Beth-Hill until the Council bound them for a hundred years. Nevertheless, a century of existence has made an indelible mark not easily forgotten for these ghostly myths that are no longer so ghostly or myth-like...

Book 1: Heart's Desire

The Wild Hunt roamed the forest outside of Beth-Hill until the Council bound them for a hundred years--a lifetime for a human but only a passing thought to one such as Gabriel, Master of the Wild Hunt. As the Council's binding draws to a close, old enemies reappear to ensure that the Wild Hunt is bound once more--to a creature much worse than the Council has been.

Publisher: http://www.writers-exchange.com/hearts-desire/

Book 2: Fire and Water

As a young vampire, Erialas Morgan brought his mother back to life with a spell that shouldn't exist, shouldn't have worked...perhaps shouldn't have been performed at all. Desperation and love are his only excuses for doing the unthinkable.

There are others who wish to use that same spell for their own gain--and to destroy the Wild Hunt once and for all. Caught in the middle of a war between the Morgan clan of vampires and their human kin, Erialas turns to the Hunt for help. But even Gabriel, the Master of Beth Wild Hunt, may not be able to stop the tide of death and destruction once it turns.

Publisher: http://www.writers-exchange.com/fire-and-water/

Book 3: The Lost

Almost sixty years ago, Darkbrook, the only school of magic in the United States, opened its doors to students of decidedly different natures, sending out letters of invitation to the elves, the dragons, and the vampires. The three who responded to the invitation banded together despite their differences but vanished only weeks later along with an entire classroom full of students and their teacher after a field trip gone horribly wrong.

The Wild Hunt has healed and the Hounds have grown closer together, keeping Darkbrook's forest safe and secure for those who live there. Malachi, one of the eldest members of the Wild Hunt, has adapted to Josiah's spell to help him see, but when a demon boy trapped in the body of a human body for sixty years inside the school disrupts the newfound calm, the Hunt--and those they protect--are thrust into a struggle that should have ended long ago when a vampire, an elf, and a dragon vanished into the Mists.

Publisher: http://www.writers-exchange.com/the-lost/

Book 4: A Glint of Silver

Jericho is a vampire who wants is to live away from the Richmond household of vampires led by his ruthless father Connor. When Jericho tries to escape, Connor punishes him and leaves him to die. Tristan is determined to be the one to bring Jericho back, but he can't see him suffer for wanting a normal life. As long as Connor lives, Jericho will never be safe or free. As long as Connor *lives*...

Publisher: http://www.writers-exchange.com/a-glint-of-silver/

Book 5: All That Glitters

As a member of the cruel Morgan Household of vampires, twelve-year-old Arthur Morgan has been abused all his life.

Maya, a water fairy, shows him just how horrible and twisted the household he's grown up is. With her help, and the unexpected help of an adult vampire, Arthur attempts to escape.

Can he become something more than what his father has decreed?

Publisher: http://www.writers-exchange.com/all-that-glitters/

The Chelsea Chronicles

Normally a quiet, serene place, Chelsea Kingdom seems like the perfect location for a centuries' old vampire to blend in and live a normal life, even escape hunters and an angry mob. Unfortunately, his timing couldn't be worse...

Book 1: So You Want to be a Vampire

Chelsea Kingdom is usually a pretty quiet place but recent murders--committed by a vampire--upset the calm. Newcomer to town, Vlad Dhalgren wants only to blend in and live a normal life. He quickly learns that isn't possible, given that other vampires have been hiding in the shadows around the castle--in plain sight--for years.

Despite her lineage, Anna Everett, the crown princess of the Kingdom of Chelsea, isn't a wizard like her father, which means she will never be Queen. She has only one friend, Valerian Moreton--Val--who has secrets he's never shared that could get him *and* Anna killed...

Publisher: http://www.writers-exchange.com/so-you-want-to-be-a-vampire/

Book 2: Transformation

As Anna, crown princess of Chelsea, adjusts to life as a vampire after recent events, Vlad plans for a future he has no real hope to seeing come to pass due to injuries sustained while attempting to save Anna's life. But, as life goes on for Anna and her friend Valerian "Val" Moreton, it changes for others--some of whom are not quite what they seem...

Publisher: http://www.writers-exchange.com/transformation/

You can find ALL our books up on our website at:

http://www.writers-exchange.com

All Jennifer's books:

http://www.writers-exchange.com/Jennifer-St-Clair/

all our fantasy novels:

http://www.writers-exchange.com/category/genres/fantasy/